Clifton an

by

Curtis Weetly

1

Delyse Joseph turned her face towards the Ocho Rios sun. Sea foam, swirled by the gentlest of warm breezes, tickled her feet. She reached down from her sun lounger. The pina colada, knocked over, had dampened the white sand. She looked around for the beach waiter. Wispy palm trees shivered in the distant heat haze. Pure blue cloudless sky met the horizon and shimmered away into distant waves. Someone called her name. She took off her sunglasses and peered along the beach. Her heart skipped, Felipe was striding towards her. What was he doing in Jamaica? His tall sculpted body glistened in the sun. A thrill of excitement as he knelt down beside her and smiled that sweet handsome smile. He caressed her bare shoulder. The caress morphed into a painful grab. Kiss me, she cried.

Delyse dragged her consciousness up from deep sleep to find Felipe's face replaced by her father's.

'Kiss you?' her father said, frowning. 'I have no intention of kissing you until I escort you to the altar.'

'Dad?' Delyse said blearily. She raised herself on to her elbows. 'I was dreaming. What's wrong?'

'You are needed at work, girl.'

'Work? Don't use bad language. This is my day off.'

'And I can tell what you did with your night off. Your bedroom smells like a Hip Strip dive.'

'This is 1985, dad, not 1885. I enjoyed a few glasses of wine with the girls.'

'I'm sure the vineyards of France are grateful for your contribution,' Eldon said. He went to the window and drew back the curtains. 'Inspector Mallick needs you on a case, urgently.'

Delyse blinked, the early morning light stinging her eyes. 'Couldn't you have told him I wasn't at home?' She took a drink of water to ease her parched throat.

'I'm not going to lie, even for you, and especially not to a fellow police officer.'

'You're no longer a police officer, dad. You're retired. I was having a lovely dream. I was back in Jamaica.'

Eldon Joseph bristled to be reminded of his retired status. 'Once a policeman, always a policeman. Besides, you're not in Jamaica now. You're in dismal England, the outskirts of Hertford.'

'I can tell from the temperature. What time is it?' Delyse looked at her bedside clock. 'It's only six thirty!' she exclaimed.

'Why do you think I'm still in my dressing gown? I'm not Noel Coward.'

'What did Mallick say? What's so urgent? Cat stuck up a tree or he needs someone to fetch his coffee?'

'He wants you to ring him as soon as possible. A suspicious death has occurred in a hotel and you're the only officer available to investigate.'

'Except I'm not available. It's my day off.' Delyse threw back the duvet and lifted her legs out of bed, glad she was wearing her old Danger Mouse pajamas.

'Where are you going?'

'Where do you think? I need the bathroom and I have to shower and brush my teeth before I go anywhere.'

'Hurry up then, Sergeant Joseph. I'll make you breakfast while you get ready. I'll also find the extra strong mints for you.'

'Don't bother with breakfast. It's far too early to eat anything. If I'm going to a hotel I'll get something there.'

'You don't know what sort of hotel you're going to. It might be a cheap seedy place. A brothel even.'

2

'Then perhaps I'll make a few quid on the side while I'm there.'

Eldon grimaced in disgust. 'Don't make filthy jokes like that, girl. What would your mother say? Ring your inspector.'

Delyse brushed past her father and into the blessed sanctuary of the bathroom. Her head thumped. She looked in the mirror. Her eyes were bloodshot. The "few glasses of wine" had been several shots of Captain Morgan rum.

'I'll make you a coffee,' Eldon said through the closed door.

'Dad! This will go faster if you don't stand outside the door. Give me some privacy.'

'Stubborn as a mule, just like your mother.' Eldon stalked off downstairs.

Delyse came downstairs feeling a little more human. She called Inspector Mallick on the hallway telephone, then went into the kitchen. Eldon, still in his dressing gown, was sitting at the kitchen table. He slid a mug of coffee towards her and said, in a disapproving tone, 'Is that what you are wearing?'

'Why? Doesn't it meet your high sartorial standards?'

'Blue jeans, T-shirt and suede jacket with a cowboy fringe is not suitable garb for a police sergeant.'

'I'm a detective, dad. We wear what we like.'

'Then why not a leather jacket over a pink tutu?' Eldon shook his head wearily. 'You are such a beautiful girl. Your mother was beautiful and graceful. She could wear a dustbin bag and still look elegant. You have been blessed with her looks and grace and yet you dress like that Rick Jagger boy.'

'It's *Mick* Jagger, dad.'

'Scruffy white boy pretending to be black. Do you want my opinion on dressing appropriately?'

3

'No, but I can see from your expression I'm about to receive the benefit of your wisdom on the matter.'

'You look at me now and you see my hair and beard turning grey, worry lines creasing my face, thickening around the waste, wearing an old dressing gown. Do you remember what I looked like when I was in the force, back in the old country?'

'I'm sure you're about to remind me.' Delyse took a sip of coffee. It was good, Jamaican Blue Mountain.

'I was always clean shaven and well-groomed. I kept my uniform immaculate. I was proud of that little crown and star on each epaulette.'

'You weren't a detective. As a Senior Superintendent you had to wear that uniform.'

'You're missing the point, Delyse. You're in a white world now. You are going to face criticism and prejudice and by dressing like a slob you are giving the racists extra ammunition. You are doubly threatened because you are female. You have an opportunity today. Your inspector has called you out. If you help him, turn up dressed immaculately to investigate this case and work it to the best of your ability you will overcome many of the unseen obstacles in your way.'

'Not all my white colleagues are racists, dad.'

'Huh,' Eldon snorted. 'They are polite to your face but what do they think behind your back? Inspector Mallick is a fellow ethnic. You should back him up. He is on your side.'

'Hardly a fellow ethnic, dad. His mother is a white English woman and his father is of Indian heritage. Mallick himself was born and brought up in England. He prefers football to cricket and bangers and mash to curry.'

'You see, even you are not above spouting racist stereotypes. Mallick is ethnic enough to make him

4

sympathetic to you. How many other black officers at your station?'

'None.'

'That's right, and I doubt there are one or two more in the entire Hertfordshire police service. You have to be a trailblazer, Delyse.'

'You don't give me much credit for what I've already achieved. I'm still the right side of thirty and I'm a sergeant. That's pretty good going.'

'I'll bet there are many more white male detective sergeants in the Hertfordshire constabulary younger than you.'

'Hertford nick is hardly a branch of the Ku Klux Klan.' Delyse shrugged. She was tired of arguing. 'Now that I've been presented with a *fait accompli*, thanks to you, I'd better get going. I'll get my bag.'

'Don't forget your notebook and your warrant card.'

Delyse went out and took down her shoulder bag from the hall stand and, despite her irritation, looked inside to make sure it contained her notebook and warrant card. She went back into the kitchen. She stroked her father's grizzled grey hair and kissed him on the forehead.

'So you're not going to change?' Eldon said.

'No, dad. Not my clothes or my attitude. I love you and I accept what you're saying but I have to get going and sometimes it's just too hard to care.' Especially with a weapons grade hangover.

'You have to care. You have to try, all the time. Do you know where this hotel is, how to get to it?'

'Yes. I'll see you later, dad.'

Delyse closed the front door and climbed into her beloved green Mini. She had no idea where the hotel was. She would get away from the house, in case her father was watching out the window, and find a layby to stop and consult her road atlas. From what Inspector Mallick had

5

told her, it sounded like the makings of an unusual case. Despite her irritation at losing her day off, she was intrigued.

2

Clifton Rossi increased his running pace for a final burn on his last circuit of Priory Park. He had a clear run as there were few other joggers and dog walkers on the embankment towpath. He glanced at his watch. Quarter past six. Plenty of time to get to work. The exercise was chasing away the last fugs of alcohol. A large mug of sweet tea and a bacon butty should complete the sobering process.

Rossi glanced at the early morning sunlight twinkling on the ripples of the River Ouse. He loved the procession of gnarled old trees along the bank. They leaned towards the water as if bowing in homage to the ancient stream. A rain shower during the night had released the comforting smells of wet earth, grass and concrete. A rowing eight glided past, like a monstrous water insect with eight long legs.

Ahead of him was Bedford Bridge. Few vehicles crossing at this hour. He made a mental note to visit his parents after work. He had not called on them for several days. After three years they had recovered from the tragic shock as well as could be expected but they still needed help and reassurance. He remembered playing cricket with his brother in this park, how fiercely competitive they were, how he hated to lose. Now he would let his brother win everything if only he were here. Rossi shook off the dark thoughts. If he allowed them to linger they would cloud his day with sorrow.

One last lung-bursting sprint took Rossi to the bridge. He stopped for several minutes, leaning forward, hands on knees, to catch his breath. Then he trudged up the grass bank and across the road towards his apartment building. A woman emerged from the courtyard entrance. Petite, elegant, short fair hair but beautifully styled. Blue eyes sparkling in the morning sun, even at distance. Light unbuttoned raincoat carelessly worn over a green dress, as chic as a Parisian model. The sight of her set his heart racing more than the running, scattered butterflies in his stomach. What was she doing here so early in the morning? Why was she carrying a suitcase? What was going on?

He walked up to her, trying to be cool, and said, 'Hello, Jane. Never thought I'd see you up and about so early. Got yourself a paper round?'

Jane smiled the wry smile he simultaneously loved and hated. 'I could say the same about you. Never thought I'd see you in running gear rather than those sharp Italian suits. Looks good. You've always had great legs.'

'Suits are not so comfortable for running but they're cheap when half the family are tailors.' Lame, lame, lame. Change the subject. He pointed at the suitcase. 'Are you going on holiday?'

A moment of awkward hesitation. 'No. I'm heading for the bus station. I'm leaving Bedford. Permanently.'

Rossi was unprepared for the stab of emotional pain this announcement caused. All he could say was, 'Oh.'

'I went up to your flat. I've put a letter through your door. I assumed you'd still be asleep at this hour, although I couldn't hear any snoring.'

'I don't snore because I don't drink any more,' Rossi lied, hoping his breath would not betray last night's painful fall off the wagon.

Jane said, 'That wasn't a dig at your drinking. I'm glad to hear you've given it up. There were three in our marriage, you, me and Johnny Walker.'

'I didn't start drinking until we broke up.'

'You know that's not true,' Jane said impatiently. 'You know full well when it really started.'

Rossi shook his head. 'Don't go there.'

'I wasn't. Just reminding you. You were always hard to understand but since "you know what" you've built an emotional stockade around your whole being and viciously repel anyone who cares about you enough to storm the barricades.'

Rossi bit back a retort. 'You're right. You look beautiful with the early morning sun on your face.'

To Rossi's surprise his compliment brought tears to Jane's eyes.

'Don't say things like that,' she said. 'We're divorced now.'

'That was your doing. Did you ever love me?'

'Of course I did. I still love you but it just doesn't work between us.'

Rossi sensed rising hope. He did not want to beat it back down. 'If you still love me and I certainly still love you then what are we doing?'

Jane ignored the question. 'The letter I left you, it was to tell you I'm moving away. And I'm getting married.'

Rossi tried to quell disappointment, and anger. 'Married? To who?'

'You don't know him. He's not a policeman. That would have been a deal breaker.'

'Where are you going?'

'The south coast. We are going to run a hotel together.'

'Dumping me for Basil Fawlty? Torquay?'

'No, Bournemouth.'

'Bournemouth! That's where fun goes to retire before it dies. Watch you don't get mown down by the zimmer frames and mobility scooters. I wouldn't be caught holidaying in Bournemouth, alive or dead, not that anyone would notice either way. How can you run a hotel when you're a lousy cook and a worse housekeeper?' Rossi immediately regretted the unfair words.

'You're lashing out, I understand that, but I won't be doing either of those jobs. I'm good at administration and organisation. I'll be working with my husband all day and every day, unlike being married to you and hardly ever seeing you. I couldn't compete with your true mistress.'

'I never cheated on you,' Rossi protested.

'I mean work. That bloody job of yours. You wouldn't give it up to save our marriage and what happened to your brother tipped us over the edge.'

'My job kept me sane. I love my job. I'm proud of what I do. I make a difference.'

'Oh, yes,' Jane said sarcastically. 'What you were really doing was competing with your brother. Detective Sergeant Clifton Rossi, once the youngest sergeant in the Bedfordshire force but that was years ago, *sergeant.* When is the next promotion coming or have you pissed that away in a whisky bottle?'

Rossi mounted a lame defence. 'It wasn't always the job that came between us. You stopped fancying me.'

'Not physically. You're tall, dark eyes, great hair, good body, Italian looks with British manners but without the British pasty look. That's an attractive package. No, I've never stopped fancying you.'

'No? Then please explain . . .'

Rossi was interrupted by his pager beeping. He took it out of his shorts pocket and checked the message. 'It's the station. I have to ring urgently.'

Jane laughed theatrically. 'Well, point proven, detective sergeant. That's what happened to us. You even take that bloody beeper out on a run. You better hurry to see what your turnip headed mates want. Goodbye, Clifton. Have a nice life.'

'No wait,' Rossi begged, but Jane was walking away. Rossi watched her until she turned the corner heading for town. They were already divorced, but this was the real ending. Dispirited, disappointed and hungover, Rossi went up to his apartment to make the call that would change his life.

3

Clifton Rossi knew the Road Star Lodge well. . .from the outside. He had driven past innumerable times in the course of his duties. It served the A1M motorway and was built, midway between the nearest towns, on the site of an abandoned petrol station, repair shop and scrap yard. It was a weather faded plain grey and white rectangular building of four storeys with a colonnaded entrance and a large garish neon sign on the roof pronouncing "Road Star Lodge" that could be seen from miles away along the ever busy motorway.

Rossi parked and went inside. He could immediately tell there were no pretensions to luxury. Judging by the foyer, it looked clean and comfortable but basic. The intended guests were weary car passengers, not holidaymakers, who needed a convenient stopover for the night. The ground floor was devoted to a restaurant, bar, exercise room and Jacuzzi and, in a one storey extension to one side, a casino. Rossi guessed the casino was where the real profits were made, and hidden.

Rossi went to the reception desk. In a quiet voice so nearby patrons could not overhear and be upset, he said to the receptionist, 'Good morning. I'm Detective Sergeant Rossi of Bedfordshire CID. I understand you have a deceased guest.'

The receptionist's bright smile turned into a grimace. She said, 'I'll get the manager.' She went into an office behind the reception desk and came out accompanied by a middle-aged man who introduced himself as the manager, Mr Farley. He was smartly dressed in grey suit and tie but looked red-faced and flustered. He said, 'Please come with me, sergeant. The body, er, the guest is on the first floor.'

As they walked up the stairs Rossi, more to make conversation than anything, asked, 'What time was the body discovered?'

'At five thirty this morning when the chambermaid entered the room.'

'That's a bit early to be waking up the guests, isn't it?'

'Mr Smith had asked to be woken up at that time.'

'Mr Smith?' Rossi said, suspecting an alias. 'I presume he was alone?'

'Yes. I checked him in myself. Very polite. He spoke good English but with quite a strong foreign accent.'

'Could you tell what nationality? Did you see any documents, passport, driving licence, credit card?'

'No I'm afraid not. He paid in cash for a one night stay. A very common procedure.'

They stepped on to the landing and turned into a long low ceilinged corridor lined with cheap framed prints and cheap carpeting. Rossi expected to see a uniformed policeman stationed outside the dead man's room but there was no-one, either police or staff or guests.

'Am I the first officer on the scene?' Rossi asked.

'I think so. I didn't come on duty until seven myself. Here it is. Room sixteen.'

'Please unlock the door.'

The manager wrung his hands. 'It's already unlocked.'

Rossi frowned. 'That's careless. Never mind, show me the body.'

'No, no,' the manager said, stepping back in panic. 'I can't go in there. I'm a bag of nerves. I'm terrified of what I might see.'

'It would be better if you accompany me,' Rossi urged. 'Then I cannot be accused of stealing anything or tampering with evidence.'

'No, no. I trust you. You're on your own.' The manager scampered back along the corridor and down the stairs.

Rossi shrugged. He searched his pockets for evidence gloves but realised that, in his hurry, he had forgotten to bring any. Using a handkerchief wrapped around his hand so as not to destroy possible fingerprints he turned the door handle. He stepped cautiously inside. An *en suite* bathroom and shower on the left. A cloakroom and storage cupboard on the right. He moved into the room. It was decorated in old fashioned 1970s pale orange and brown tones, including the curtains, and furnished with cheap blonde wood furniture. He glanced at the body which, covered with a white sheet, lay on the double bed. To his amazement a woman, her back towards him, was opening one of the drawers in the dressing table.

Rossi said loudly, 'Madam, this is a crime scene. You have no right to be in here. Put back whatever you have stolen otherwise I will arrest you for theft and interfering with the course of justice.'

To Rossi's surprise the woman turned around looking neither startled nor perturbed. She said, 'That's a pompous way of putting things. I suppose you think, because I'm black, that I'm stealing. Who are you?'

'Who are *you*?'

'I asked first and, if you're about to arrest me, I have the right to know.'

'I am Detective Sergeant Rossi of Bedfordshire CID.'

The woman crossed her arms defiantly. 'Show me your warrant card.'

Rossi felt in all his pockets and realised that, along with the plastic gloves, he had forgotten to bring his warrant card.

The woman smiled. 'All those pockets in that sharp suit and no room for your warrant card.' She moved towards a shoulder bag laying on the bed.

'Be careful,' Rossi warned.

14

The woman picked up the bag. 'Don't worry, sergeant. I haven't got a gun in here. It's something much more effective.' She took out a warrant card and handed it to Rossi.

Rossi read aloud, 'Detective Sergeant Delyse Joseph of Hertfordshire CID.' He gave back the card. 'Why are you here?'

'Firstly, I'm going to arrest you for impersonating a police officer. Secondly, I am investigating the death of that poor soul under the sheet. This is a Hertfordshire case. That's what I'm doing here. This hotel is in Hertfordshire.'

'On the contrary, the address is Bedfordshire.'

'Either way,' Delyse said, 'you are not supposed to be here at the crime scene. No identification, no investigation for you.'

Rossi was stung and embarrassed. 'Do you expect me to believe you're actually a detective when you're dressed like Calamity Jane? Is the Wild West this year's *de rigueur* look for Hertfordshire detectives?' Rossi fully realised he was making up criticism to save face.

'I had to leave in a hurry this morning,' Delyse replied, trying not to look ruffled by Rossi's sarcasm. 'The fact remains that I have a warrant card and you do not. This is a Hertfordshire CID case. Please don't touch anything and leave the room.'

As Delyse spoke a senior uniformed officer unexpectedly entered the room. He was tall and slim and, although he wore his hat at an almost a jaunty angle, he radiated confidence and authority. He said, 'Good morning, Sergeant Rossi. What's going on?'

'Thank goodness,' Rossi said. He turned to Delyse and told her, 'This is Chief Superintendent Pritchard of Bedfordshire constabulary. Sir, this is Detective Sergeant Joseph of Hertfordshire CID. Unfortunately I forgot to

15

bring my warrant card so she doesn't believe who I am. Please tell her I'm a legitimate officer, sir.'

Pritchard grinned jovially. 'Forgotten your warrant card, sergeant? That's a very serious offence. I think a written reprimand is in order.'

Rossi sighed. 'I'll accept any punishment you think fit but please tell this woman that I am a legitimate detective.'

Delyse said, 'This "woman" is a detective sergeant, if you please.'

'It does not please me but apparently we've both been called out to the same case.'

'Yes, indeed,' Pritchard said. 'I was on my way to the office when I heard on the radio that both counties had been called out so I decided to stop by and clear things up. The interesting thing is that this hotel straddles the border between Bedfordshire and Hertfordshire and the manager tells me the county line runs right through the middle of this very room. Isn't that amusing?'

'Not for that poor guy under the sheet,' Delyse said.

'You are correct, sergeant,' Pritchard said, chastened. 'The actual address is a Bedfordshire address but the postcode is Hertfordshire, hence the mix-up, but I have some good news. As you two sergeants are here on the spot, you are both authorised to investigate this suspicious death. Sergeant Joseph, I've contacted your superiors and cleared the arrangement with their agreement. It will be a valuable exercise in cross county teamwork and co-operation.'

Delyse, horrified, said, 'I protest, sir. I do not wish to work with this man. Despite dressing like someone out of *The Godfather* himself, he has already made derogatory remarks about the way I'm dressed.'

Rossi bristled. 'This is a handmade suit, unlike your C and A buckskin jacket.'

'It's suede, you moron. Sir, this sort of forcible stitch-up is not how things are done.'

16

Pritchard pointed to his epaulette. 'You see this pip and this crown. These denote that things are done how I tell you to do them.' He stepped over to the bed and raised the sheet to look at the dead man's face. 'He looks almost serene.' He replaced the sheet and said, 'I'll leave you to it. I, and your superiors, Sergeant Joseph, expect a full report as soon as possible.'

Pritchard walked out of the room but Rossi followed. Further along the corridor, out of earshot, Rossi whispered, 'Sir, may I have a word with you?'

Pritchard, exasperated, turned around. 'What is it?'

'Sir, you cannot make me work with that woman.'

'Why not?'

'I don't know what she's like. I don't know her working methods.'

'You'll have to give me a better reason than that, sergeant.'

'I'm used to working with male officers,' Rossi said in desperation. 'You know, the camaraderie, talking about football and telly and whistling at girls.'

'You should not be harassing women in that manner. You'll still have to do better.'

Rossi took a deep breath. 'Very well,' he said. 'She's black.'

Pritchard's eyes widened. 'Are you admitting to being a racist, sergeant?'

'No, not as such, but I don't know what to say to her, how to behave.'

'Like a normal human being I should think.'

'But you know how it is, sir. You say one word out of place, use the wrong expression and you're facing an accusation of prejudice or discrimination.'

'Then you had better watch what you say, sergeant. Now, get on with it, I won't hear another word.'

17

Rossi watched Pritchard disappear and then trudged back to the hotel room.

'What happened there?' Delyse asked rhetorically.

'Chief Superintendent Pritchard is a Welshman with a wry sense of humour and loves putting one over on the English. He thinks it's a great joke to make us work together.'

'Maybe, but that's not what I meant. Why does a uniformed senior officer unexpectedly visit the scene of a routine unexplained death and pull a stunt like making us work together?'

'Pritchard likes to think he's a comedian, Bedford's answer to Ken Dodd. That's why I followed him, to try to change his mind.'

'That's not why,' Delyse said dismissively. 'You told him you don't want to work with a black person, didn't you?'

'No, of course not.'

'I see it every time when I'm partnered with another white male, and I'm surrounded by white males. They either hate me because of my skin colour or they're coming on to me because they think black girls are easy. So don't you try it because I live with a bloke and he's black. I don't go with white men.'

'Don't worry, I have no intention of either hating you or "coming on" to you. I'm afraid you'll analyse and suspect everything I do and say while we're working together and end up branding me a racist if I say one word out of place.'

'It works both ways. I'm afraid you might bad mouth me to our superiors, however well I do, just because of the colour of my skin.'

'Listen, I know all about prejudice. I'm half Italian and half English. I feel completely English but I was called every name at school. Wop, eyetie, pasta muncher. See, even you are smiling at that insult.'

'I'm smiling because you can hardly compare your experience in Bedford, which is full of people of Italian heritage, with my situation as a black woman of Jamaican heritage transferring to the leafy English suburbs of Hertfordshire.'

Rossi thought about telling Delyse about his brother as an example of real prejudice but he was tiring of the whole conversation, the whole situation. 'Why don't we concentrate on finding out why that poor sod under the sheet is dead? Maybe we're worrying over nothing. Perhaps we won't have to put up with each other for more than a few hours. Perhaps it's simply natural causes and not suspicious at all.'

'Okay, that's fair comment,' Delyse said, 'but unless our cadaver is a naturist and checked into the hotel stark naked without any luggage then circumstances are highly suspicious.'

'What do you mean?' Rossi asked, baffled.

'Before you barged in and tried to arrest me I had looked through the dresser drawers, the bedside cabinets and the closet. There are no clothes, no luggage, no personal effects of any kind. The room has been stripped of any form of identification.'

Rossi felt he had to look for himself while Delyse, shaking her head in disgust, watched him. After he had repeated her search he said, 'I've heard of travelling light but this is ridiculous. Strangest crime scene I've ever attended.'

'I've also searched for signs of blood and for signs of a fight or physical struggle. There is nothing.' Delyse took out a pair of plastic evidence gloves from her bag. 'Let's take this sheet off and examine the body.'

'I didn't bring any gloves,' Rossi admitted.

Delyse sighed theatrically, savouring another small victory, and handed Rossi a pair. They gently removed the bedsheet and looked at the body. He was in a supine position with arms by his side as if laying to attention.

Delyse said, 'Male, middle-aged, with . . .'

'I'd say more mid-to-late thirties.' Rossi said. 'He looks pretty fit.'

'Okay, agreed. Tall, about your height, say six feet. Thick brown hair, nose looks as if it might have been broken at some point, thin lips, not very carefully shaven. Mole on his chest but can't see any other distinguishing features like tattoos or scars. Impossible to say what nationality but odds on he's British.'

'Perhaps not. The manager said he spoke good English but with a pronounced accent. Let's turn him over.'

They looked at each other to express unspoken distaste at the prospect.

'Okay,' Delyse said. 'Has to be done.'

They slid their arms under the torso and rolled the corpse on to his side. Rossi grabbed the shoulder, before the corpse could topple back, and shoved him the rest of the way into a prone position.

'Here's something,' Rossi said. 'Something fallen into the gap between the bedside cabinet and the bed.' He gingerly retrieved the object. A pair of tortoiseshell spectacles. He examined them. 'They look ordinary. No name, just a small eagle-like emblem or logo on the frame.' He handed them to Delyse.

Delyse nodded. 'I'll leave them on the pillow next to him for when forensics collect his personal effects.'

'That'll be a quick job.'

They studied the body.

Rossi pointed. 'There's a small scar here above his left buttock. Could be an old knife wound. I can't see any evidence of what might have killed him. No bullet wounds, knife wounds, signs of strangulation or defence wounds.'

'There's only one other thing I can think of,' Delyse said. 'I'll look for puncture marks from a hypodermic needle.' She gently prized open the toes of the corpse, then his fingers, and looked behind the ear flaps. 'Nothing. You do his bum.'

'What?' Rossi spluttered. 'What do you mean?'

'I mean prize apart the cheeks of his bum and look for needle marks.'

'Not on your life. You do it if you're that keen.'

'It wouldn't be decorous or respectful for me, a woman, to do it.'

'You're just using that as an excuse.'

They stared at each other.

'You're right,' Delyse finally admitted. 'This is definitely a suspicious death so we should get forensics here and leave any prodding and poking to the pathologist.'

'Agreed. Shall we call out Bedfordshire or Hertfordshire forensics?'

'Let's use my guys. They are very good and they will be intrigued by this crime scene. No blood, no mess, no clothes, no nothing.'

A knock on the door. Rossi went to open it. The manager, Mr Farley, stood there wringing his hands. He said, 'May I ask what's going on? Is it a murder? My head office will need to be informed.'

Delyse joined them. Rossi introduced Delyse and explained that they would be working together on the case.

Delyse said, 'We're not sure about murder but the death is definitely suspicious. All the deceased's clothes and personal effects have been removed. Would you or your staff have done that?'

'Heavens no! We have a strict policy about inspecting, touching or stealing things from our guests.'

'I should hope so,' Rossi said. 'Okay. We have to find out who removed the deceased's personal effects. We'll have to compile a list of all staff and guests who were in the hotel since the deceased checked in and interview them all.'

Delyse nodded. 'We'll need uniforms as back up to do that.'

'Yes. It's essential to know who has been in and out of this room in the past few hours. Mr Farley, can you assemble your staff and arrange that please?'

The manager looked baffled. 'I could, but why not just watch the film?'

Rossi and Delyse looked at each other. 'What film?' Delyse asked.

The manager pointed to a security camera at the end of the corridor.

4

The Road Star Lodge "security suite" was actually one cramped room situated in the casino wing. The state-of-the-art security equipment consisted of one large television screen and one VHS tape player. Delyse and Rossi sat side by side and disconsolately stared at the screen. It was blank, unstarted.

Rossi said, 'A fine pair of detectives we are. Right plonkers not to notice the security cameras.'

'What's a plonker?' Delyse asked.

'Don't you watch much television? It's what Del Boy calls his brother in *Only Fools and Horses.*'

'I've never watched it.'

'You don't know what you're missing. What programmes do you watch?'

'Not many. Educational and travel documentaries mainly. I don't enjoy watching white people trying to be funny. I can't relate.'

'Try Lenny Henry. He's black and brilliant.'

Delyse decided it was time to change the subject. 'Who would have thought a roach pit like this place would spend money on an up-to-the-minute security system when they haven't changed the décor since last decade?'

Rossi nodded. 'It's made our job a lot easier. We just have to watch the tape recording from the time our victim entered the hotel room until we see whatever miscreants coming out with all his belongings. We can fast forward the tape so this shouldn't take long. Press play.'

'Yes, boss.'

They watched the victim arrive and unlock the door to enter the room. He was unaccompanied, carrying his own luggage, a single large suitcase.

'The manager told me they don't have official bell boys,' Rossi commented.

'Film's obviously not in colour,' Delyse said, 'but that's a light suit he's wearing. Fawn, tan, light grey, something like that. Nothing unusual.'

'He's not wearing his spectacles either.'

'There's another possibility.'

'What?'

'That the spectacles belong to whoever stole his belongings and did not belong to the victim.'

'The thief would surely have come back to retrieve them.'

'Perhaps he or she couldn't find them. They had fallen between bed and nightstand.'

'Um,' Rossi said. They watched the tape speeding past for a few minutes, then he said, 'I'm starving. And thirsty. Do you fancy a coffee? I'll go rustle up a couple of mugs while you watch that.'

'Okay. Get me a bacon butty. I could do with a reviver.'

'Heavy night last night?'

'Not particularly,' Delyse lied.

Rossi realised that Delyse was not going to elaborate so he left the room.

Twenty minutes later Rossi returned with coffees and bacon butties. 'Found anything?' he asked.

'Yes. Nothing.'

'What do you mean, nothing?

'Philosophically, nothing means the complete absence of anything.'

'Christ, I bet you were the teacher's pet at school. There must be something!'

Delyse ignored the barb. 'We saw the victim enter the room, yes?'

'Yes.'

Delyse rewound the tape. 'Here is the chambermaid entering the room at just after five thirty. Seconds later she exits looking distressed and shocked. Between the victim entering and the maid running out in tears, that door never opened.'

'It must have done!' Rossi protested. 'You must have missed it. Did you nod off or nip out to the loo or something?'

Delyse snorted contemptuously.

Rossi said, 'I have to see for myself. Run the tape again.'

Delyse threw up her hands in exasperation. 'Again you don't believe me. You don't trust me. You had to search the hotel room after I told you everything had gone, now you think I can't watch a tape without messing up.'

Rossi shifted irritably. 'I have to see for myself.'

Delyse shrugged and fully rewound the tape. They sat silently, eating and sipping coffee, watching the frames whizzing past on the screen. Eventually Delyse pressed stop. 'Well, did you see anyone leave that room?'

'No,' Rossi admitted.

They sat in silence for several minutes. Then Delyse lifted the receiver of the internal phone and asked for the manager. 'Would you ask the chambermaid who found the body, Miss Piper I think you said, to come to the security suite?'

'What are you thinking?' Rossi asked as Delyse put down the receiver.

'If the personal effects were not taken out via the door there is only one other possibility.'

A few minutes later there was a knock on the door. Rossi got up and opened it. 'Are you Miss Piper?'

Miss Piper blushed. 'Yes. Am I in any trouble?'

'No, no. My colleague has a question for you.'

25

Miss Piper was a big built girl, shy and awkward, but she had a kind face, peachy complexion, sparkling eyes and obviously kept herself neat and tidy and well-groomed.

Rossi pulled out his chair and invited Miss Piper to sit down while he remained standing. Miss Piper smiled at him and blushed again.

Delyse began, 'It must have been a shock to discover the body. You have my sympathy. I'm afraid we have to ask a couple of questions. Are you sure the body was completely naked when you went in?'

'Yes. You could see his willy and everything.'

Rossi stopped himself from laughing by putting a hand over his mouth. A sour look from Delyse helped.

Delyse went on. 'Did you see any other personal effects when you were in the room?'

'No, nothing, and I didn't take anything either. I'm not like that.'

Rossi said, 'Don't worry, Miss Piper. You are not under any suspicion. We're just trying to find out what happened to that poor man.'

Miss Piper smiled at Rossi gratefully.

Delyse asked, 'When you went in, did you notice whether the curtains were drawn or open?'

Miss Piper became flustered. 'I don't know. I can't remember. No, wait, it was beginning to get light. Yes, the curtains were open.'

'And the windows, can they be opened from outside?'

'No, you have to press a button on the inside to unlock the windows for cleaning and so on. Then they lock automatically when closed again.'

'Were any of the big windows open?'

'No, I'm sure they weren't. I'd have noticed that. Did you see who did it on the tape?'

Delyse said, 'I'm afraid we can't divulge any information at this stage but the security tapes have been extremely useful.'

Miss Piper grinned. 'That's great because I urged the management to install the camera system. My uncle is a surveillance specialist and gave them a good price to do the work. He'll be delighted to know we've helped a police enquiry.'

Rossi said, 'That shows commendable initiative, Miss Piper.'

'You can call me Sandra.'

'Thank you, Sandra. You've been a big help. We'll let you get back to your duties.'

'Let me know if you want to see me again. Anytime.' Sandra left the office after a last shy glance at Rossi. He closed the door.

Delyse was smiling. 'Smoothly done, Romeo.'

'What are you talking about?'

'Don't tell me you are unaware the effect your macho Italian charm had on Miss Piper. She was coming on to you so hard you almost collided.'

Rossi waved a dismissive hand. 'You're imagining things. Let's get back to work. So the personal effects could have been taken out of the window but the windows could only have been opened by the victim.'

'That's how it seems. Looks like you need to cool down after your steamy encounter with Miss Piper. Let's go outside and see if there are any clues to be found.'

They left the casino and walked around to the back of the main building to a position below the victim's room. A rough grass area ran up to the brickwork.

'Yes, look,' Rossi pointed. 'It rained last night so the ground is soft. Two deep indents where a ladder was placed.'

'Plenty of footprints in this dirt. I think there were two people involved here, maybe even three.'

Rossi looked around. 'No security cameras. No automatic security lights to come on. Only fields for a few hundred yards until those farm buildings beyond the trees. Someone could easily have removed the personal belongings this way without being seen.'

'Very risky though. The big question is why someone would book into a hotel room then open the windows for someone to climb in by ladder and take away all his belongings.'

'I don't think the victim realised he was going to be robbed and killed. He must have known the assailants to have let them in. I think he was murdered and then his belongings removed.'

Delyse shook her head doubtfully. 'In that case, who closed and locked the windows? We must tell the forensics team about this evidence out here. They'll take casts of those footprints. I'll ask them to pay special attention to the windows for fingerprinting.'

'We can't do much more until we find out who this guy was. Hopefully the post mortem will give us some answers. In the meantime we should go back to our respective stations and report. We can liaise by phone until the autopsy results are available.'

'That'll be a relief for you,' Delyse said wryly. 'Get away from the black girl nuisance.'

'And for you I should think, to get away from the cut-price Mafia Romeo.'

5

Rossi parked his car on the road outside Delyse's house. The house was situated in a village three miles north of Hertford in a pleasant leafy side road leading off the main road through the village. The house was not what Rossi had expected. It was semi-detached with bow fronted windows on the ground floor and, from its style, looked to have been built in the 1930s. The front garden was neatly kept behind a low brick wall and a screen of well-trimmed bushes. There was a small conservatory on the side but no garage.

Rossi was surprised to see Delyse's Mini still parked in the drive. He had expected her to have left for the autopsy report by now. He was not sure why he had taken a detour to view her house. He told himself he was simply being nosey, curious as to how she lived. On a whim he got out of the car, walked up the short drive and rang the front door bell. After a minute Eldon Joseph opened the door, leaving it ajar on the security chain, and looked out suspiciously.

Rossi said, 'Hello, sir. I'm looking for Delyse Joseph.'

'Why? Who are you?'

'I'm Delyse's colleague, Detective Sergeant Rossi from Bedfordshire CID.'

Eldon looked Rossi up and down critically. 'Show me your warrant card.'

Rossi took out his warrant card and handed it to the old man. Eldon scrutinised it carefully and handed it back. 'What do you want?' he asked.

'I've come to offer Delyse a lift. We have to attend an autopsy report in about half an hour.'

'I know,' Eldon nodded, opening the door wider. 'Not a nice duty. I've attended quite a few in my time. I'm

Delyse's father. You had better come in.' Eldon closed the door and shouted up the stairs. 'Delyse! Your lift is here.'

'What lift?' Delyse called back.

'Your colleague, Sergeant Ross. Smart, well-dressed chap in a suit and tie. A credit to his force.'

'Thank you but my name is Rossi, actually. I'm of mixed English and Italian descent.'

Delyse shouted down, 'Tell him I don't need a lift. I can make my own way.'

Eldon called, 'The sergeant has come out of his way to pick you up. It doesn't make sense to use two cars and it will be good for you to have some moral support. Now dress yourself smartly, girl, and do your duty.' Eldon turned to Rossi. 'Come and wait in the living room.'

Rossi followed Eldon into a pleasantly light and airy open plan room. Rossi could see a substantial well-kept garden beyond the French windows.

'Lovely house and location you have here, Mr Joseph.'

'Thank you.' He ushered Rossi to sit in an armchair.

'Do I take it that you were in the police force, Mr Joseph?'

'Indeed I was, but in Jamaica. Senior Superintendent. Interesting and unusual case you and Delyse have here.'

'Yes, but I'm afraid I'm not allowed to discuss details.'

'No need, sergeant. Delyse has told me everything. Naked man found in a hotel room but all his clothes and personal belongings removed by person or persons unknown.'

'Well, as I said, I'm really not allowed to go into . . .'

'The spectacles are interesting. I came across such a pair many years ago in Kingston. Should help you establish the victim's nationality.'

Despite himself, Rossi was intrigued. 'How do you mean?'

'The eagle symbol engraved on the ear pieces. I've seen it before.'

Before Rossi could find out more Delyse entered the room, her anger unconcealed. She glared at Rossi and demanded, 'What are you doing here?'

'I thought I'd stop by and offer you a lift.'

'How did you find out where I live?'

'I'm a detective. It's not rocket science.'

'I don't want a lift. Please go. I'll meet you at the pathology department.'

Eldon said, 'Don't be so rude on the man. Let him drive you.' He checked what Delyse was wearing, a navy blue suit with a white blouse and her mother's elegant solitaire diamond necklace. 'You look very suitable. Now, remember what I told you and you'll earn some credit from your white bosses. No offence, Sergeant Rossi.'

'None taken,' Rossi smiled, more at the expression on Delyse's face than her father's remark.

'Oh, come on then,' Delyse said. She stormed out, picking up her shoulder bag from the hallstand, with Rossi in her wake.

As soon as the front door closed, Delyse said angrily, 'I don't believe you. Are you stalking me?'

'Stalking you! Don't flatter yourself. Although you do look hot in that suit in a scary schoolmarm way.'

'Now you're coming on to me. In your dreams, sergeant. Is this your car?'

Rossi held out his hand to introduce his beloved. 'This isn't just a car, Delyse. This is a Lancia Delta Integrale in Ferrari red.' He opened the passenger door for Delyse to get in.

As Rossi started the engine Delyse said, 'This is your boy toy, isn't it. Does it compensate for a tiny dick? Do you expect to attract "the ladies" with this thing?'

'I don't need a car to attract the ladies,' Rossi said, turning the Lancia on to the main road. 'When you said you lived with a bloke, I didn't think you meant your father. When he opened the door I thought he was a bit too old for you. Maybe not.'

Delyse shifted uncomfortably. 'I told you I lived with someone so you wouldn't get any ideas. I don't fancy white men.'

Rossi whistled. 'Wow, no racism there. What if I said I don't fancy black girls?'

'I'd say lucky for them.'

There was an uncomfortable silence for a few moments.

'Okay,' Rossi said. 'Let's call a truce and be professional. Have you had any more thoughts about the case?'

'I have some ideas, which I'll save for the post mortem.'

'Intriguing. Do you always freeze out your working partners?' Delyse did not respond so Rossi continued. 'The forensics report was a big disappointment. Dozens of fingerprints, which you would expect from a hotel room. The prints taken from around the window frames didn't match any known perps.'

'And they had no blood to work with. Perhaps the dental records at the post mortem might reveal something.'

'I doubt it. Dental records are useful to confirm someone's identity but when there is no clue about identity in the first place they are not much use. Any other thoughts?'

'One thing my father said has given me pause for thought, something we've already talked about.'

'What's that?'

'Your Chief Superintendent who put us together on this case.'

'Pritchard? What about him?'

'Why should an officer of his rank turn up, in full uniform, early at an incident which was not clearly a murder but could have been a quite usual unexpected death? Chief Supers are usually glorified administrators who don't get involved with anything less than the most serious cases. That's what my dad thought, anyway.'

'Umm, I see your point but I wouldn't read too much into it. As I've said, Pritchard is a maverick with a peculiar sense of humour. He's also Welsh and enjoys irritating the English. It's just the sort of thing he loves to do. Turn up unexpectedly at an ordinary incident and think it amusing to put us together and watch us squabble. Aside from that he's a bloody good copper. He's helped me out, given me a leg up more than once.'

'I'll take your word for it. Take a right at this roundabout and follow the signs to the hospital. That's where the mortuary is.'

'Handy,' Rossi said.

6

Rossi and Delyse walked along a gloomy windowless basement corridor, footsteps echoing off tiled walls, towards the mortuary and pathology lab. Outside the laboratory a man was pacing up and down. As they approached he said impatiently, 'You two are late. Mr Stroud was ready ten minutes ago.'

Before Delyse could stop him, Rossi said pugnaciously, 'Who the hell are you?'

Delyse put her hand on Rossi's arm and said to the man, 'Sorry, boss. This is Sergeant Rossi from Bedfordshire CID. Clifton, this is my boss, Inspector Mallick.'

'I didn't realise any of our superiors would be here,' Rossi said tartly, looking at Delyse accusingly.

'Inspector Mallick informed me earlier today that he would be attending the post mortem report at the request of your Chief Superintendent Pritchard.'

'Sounds like we're not trusted to do our job,' Rossi said.

'No need to get snippy,' Mallick replied, trying to mollify Rossi. 'I've got plenty of better things to do than be here.' He took a deep breath. 'These autopsies are never pleasant. Let's calm down. I'm here to help, Sergeant Rossi, not spy on you.'

Mallick was a middle-aged man, medium build, wearing a brown suit and Hush Puppies, with an owlish expression emphasised by spectacles. His hair, the only concession to vanity, was thick, black and wavy. Rossi, despite his annoyance, formed the impression that Mallick was a reasonable man. He sensed Delyse liked him as well.

Mallick went on, 'Before we go in, have you two had any more thoughts on this case.'

'Yes, sir,' Delyse said promptly. 'I believe the victim is Russian or eastern European from the Soviet Union.'

Rossi looked at Delyse in amazement but decided to say nothing.

'How did you reach that conclusion?' Mallick said.

'His spectacles. They bear a small eagle symbol. I did a lot of research and found it's the symbol of a company named Opnah. It's a state-controlled industry making spectacles and other optical devices for use in the USSR and Soviet Empire. They do not sell to the outside world because their products are pretty cheap and crude compared with Western opticals.'

Mallick nodded. 'That's good work, Delyse. Let's go in and see if the pathologist can support your theory.'

As they entered the laboratory Rossi whispered to Delyse, 'Teachers pet.'

Delyse ignored him. They walked through the research lab and into the mortuary section. The corpse of the Road Star victim was under a white sheet on a metal dissection table in the centre of the room. Cold white strip lighting illuminated the white walls, the steel and aluminium cabinets and instruments. There were no windows. In an adjoining room were floor to ceiling metal drawers containing the mortuary's customers. Delyse tried not to shudder. She looked at Rossi and saw that he was pale and tense, trying not to let the situation overwhelm him.

The pathologist, Mr Stroud, was a tall, slim man wearing a white lab coat and a bow tie. At first Rossi thought the bow tie looked like an affectation but then reflected that perhaps an ordinary tie got in the way of Stroud's grisly work. Stroud was at least sixty years old but still had a fairly thick head of hair turning distinguished grey around the edges. 'Welcome,' he said, after the introductions. 'A very interesting case we have here. You said the body was found

35

without any clothing or personal effects whatsoever, except the spectacles.'

'That's right,' Mallick said.

'So you have no clue who this person is?'

'No, sir,' Mallick said.

'Well, I can give you a good guess as to his nationality. He's. . .'

'Russian,' Delyse interrupted.

Stroud frowned and looked annoyed at having his big reveal spoiled, but he said, 'Well done, young lady.'

'I'm a Detective Sergeant.'

'Of course. My apologies. What makes you think he is Russian?'

'His spectacles are of a type manufactured only in Russia for sale throughout the Soviet Union.' Delyse explained her reasoning further.

'Well,' Stroud said, trying to regain the initiative. 'We cannot be absolutely sure the glasses belonged to the victim. They could belong to one of his assailants.'

'*One* of his assailants,' Rossi queried. 'Do you think there was more than one murderer?'

'Yes, there was surely two or more to be able to remove all his belongings out of the window, and the manner of his murder suggests at least two people held him down.'

'So you've established how he was killed?' Rossi said.

'Yes. You may remember a few years ago that a dissident journalist named Georgi Markov, Bulgarian I think, was assassinated with a poison-tipped umbrella. The poison is called ricin. It's derived from a plant usually used to make castor oil. In a purified form, a few grains of ricin, like table salt, are deadly when injected. Our poor victim here was injected with a lethal dose.'

'We looked for puncture wounds,' Delyse said. 'We couldn't find any.'

'Perhaps you didn't look in the place that no-one would care to look. He was injected near his anus. The mark was so small that you probably wouldn't have noticed it anyway.' Stroud was regaining the high ground of knowledge.

Rossi said, 'I did look there. You're right, it was too small to notice.'

Delyse looked at him and gently shook her head at his lie.

Rossi went on: 'Would this ricin stuff have killed the victim immediately?'

'It works quickly,'Stroud replied, 'but the victim would still have a few minutes before he suffered the full effects.'

'So he would have had time to close and lock the windows.'

'Oh yes,' Stroud said. 'His stomach contents were normal except he had drunk a good quantity of vodka. Another pointer to a Russian connection.'

Delyse said, 'If he was drunk when he checked into the hotel the staff didn't notice and he looked sober enough on the security camera tapes.'

'Okay,' Mallick said, 'we know how he died but we are no nearer establishing his identity. Did you check his dental records, Mr Stroud?'

'Nothing and no-one to check them against. I have prepared X-ray photographs of his teeth in case we find an identity.' Stroud went to a side table and picked up a large envelope. 'You'll find them in here with the fingerprints and the full autopsy report. Also I have taken photographs of the victim's face in case you find anyone who might be able to identify him. Normally I would give you a bag containing his personal effects but there are only the spectacles.'

'We'll take those as well,' Delyse said.

'Of course,' Stroud said. 'If I can be of any further assistance then let me know and I'll contact you if I think of anything else. You might want to take those photographs and dental records down to the Soviet embassy. They might have someone missing or perhaps could help you identify the victim. It's quite normal for embassies to co-operate in identifying deceased extra-nationals.'

The three police officers left the mortuary and walked out to the hospital car park for several deep breaths of fresh air and welcome light, life and sunshine.

Mallick said, 'I think it's a good idea for you two to visit the Soviet embassy and see if you can dig up anything. Good to meet you, Sergeant Rossi. Delyse, no point coming back to the station, it's too late. Take the rest of the day off. I'll see you whenever but keep in touch.' He climbed in his car and drove away.

Rossi said airily, 'I quite fancy a trip to London. What about you?'

'I'm intrigued to find out the identity of our victim now we have the Russian connection.'

'That was a smart move you pulled with Mallick, showing you knew the victim was Russian before the pathologist revealed it.'

'I have to be smart in my situation.'

'Stroud the Shroud was quite put out that you knew as much as him, but you didn't do all that research as you claimed. It was your dad who knew about the eagle emblem on the spectacles.'

Delyse smiled. 'Good old daddy.'

Rossi laughed. 'I hope Mallick gives you the brownie points for that initiative. If he's like most of my superiors he'll take the credit himself.'

'Mallick is a fair bloke. He'll give me my credit.'

'I hope you're right. I'll pop back into the hospital and ring Chief Superintendent Pritchard, get his permission for our trip to London, and claim the expenses. Do you like London?'

'It's a fascinating city but I wouldn't want to live there.'

'I would. I'd like a penthouse flat overlooking the river and join the Sweeney.'

Delyse looked baffled.

'It's Cockney rhyming slang,' Rossi said. 'Sweeney Todd, Flying Squad. Regan and Carter. Get your coat, you're nicked. You've no idea what I'm talking about. You really should watch more television.'

7

Rossi steered the Lancia in to the Josephs' drive and switched off the engine.

'What are you doing?' Delyse asked. 'I thought you were dropping me off, then turning around and going back to whatever slum you inhabit in Bedfordshire.'

'I have a proposition,' Rossi said. 'Pritchard gave me permission to claim expenses for an overnight stay in a hotel. Instead of that, why don't I sleep in your house and we split the expenses?'

Delyse regarded him with astonishment. 'Are you completely mad? Not only would I not let you sleep in my house, I'm not going to take a share of illicit hotel expenses. It's unscrupulous, immoral and probably illegal.'

'Come on, Del, we could get an early start and an early train to London together.'

'Absolutely not. And don't call me Del. Now go!'

'At least let me say hello to your father and thank him for his tip about the spectacles.'

'Why? There's no need for that.'

'A man's ego is wrapped up in what he does for a living, how useful he feels. Your dad has made a significant contribution to our case. It would give him a fillip to be thanked and to talk to a fellow copper who isn't his daughter. He must feel isolated and unwanted sometimes.'

'Oh, you're good,' Delyse said sarcastically. 'That's really low, playing on my feelings of guilt. All right, you can come in for five minutes and talk to dad, then you go home. Is that clear?'

'Crystal.'

They went into the house. Eldon Joseph was in the kitchen making a pot of tea. He looked at Rossi warily. 'Hello, sergeant. I didn't expect to see you again.'

Delyse said, 'Clifton wanted to thank you for your information about the spectacles. The post mortem strongly suggested the victim was a Russian.'

'Did you get a solid identification?'

'No,' Rossi said. 'We're going to the Soviet Union embassy tomorrow to see if they can identify the victim from fingerprints and post mortem photographs. Your daughter cannily used your information to gain some credit with her boss, who turned up for the report. The pathologist was mightily impressed as well.'

Eldon grinned. 'Well done, girl. Show the man you can do the job better than any . . . anyone else.'

Delyse said, 'Thanks, dad.' She turned to Rossi. 'Thanks for popping in. I'll show you to the front door now.'

Eldon said, 'Wait a minute. I'm making a pot of tea. Perhaps the sergeant would like a cup.'

'That would be most welcome, sir. Milk, no sugar, thanks.'

'No sugar, eh. You look as if you take care of yourself. The usual two spoonfuls for Delyse.' Eldon arranged the cups on a tray and said, 'Come on into the living room.'

Delyse said, 'A quick cup of tea then I'll get your dinner, dad.'

As they filed into the living room Rossi looked at the television and cried, 'Great! You've got the cricket on!'

'Yes,' Eldon said, setting down the tray on the coffee table. 'It's the second Test at Edgbaston. Do you like cricket, sergeant?'

'I love it,' Rossi said as they settled into armchairs. 'Please call me Clifton.'

'Don't you mean Clifford?'

'No, my mother was born in the village of Clifton in Bedfordshire and chose that as my given name.'

'Do you play cricket yourself?' Eldon asked.

Delyse sighed with exasperation as she realised this was not going to be a brief conversation.

'I certainly do,' Rossi said, 'for Bedfordshire police team. I'm a handy mid-order batsman and a decent swing bowler. Fielding could do with improvement. I try to emulate Ian Botham.'

Eldon laughed. 'Well, Beefy is about the only player who could get into the current West Indies team.'

Rossi smiled. 'I hate to admit it but you're right. I bet you're going to gloat about the "whitewash" drubbing the Windies gave us last year.'

Eldon laughed again. 'I wouldn't be as rude as to bring up the subject but we gave you a hell of a beating in the Test matches.'

'There's talk of that Windies team being the greatest team of all time. Fabulous batsmen, Lloyd, Richards, Greenidge, and even better bowlers, Holding, Garner, Marshall, Walsh.'

'I couldn't argue with the greatest label.'

Delyse startled when Eldon and Rossi shouted simultaneously as an Australian stump cartwheeled down the pitch. They spent the next few minutes discussing the relative strengths and weaknesses of the England Test team.

Rossi put down his cup and saucer. 'Well, I better be going. Long drive back to Bedford. It's a pity I'll miss the end with the match so well poised.'

'Stay and have dinner with us,' Eldon said.

'I don't think Delyse would like that,' Rossi said, glancing at Delyse's horrified expression.

'Nonsense,' Eldon said. 'I don't get to talk cricket very often. Delyse is not keen on the sport. She's a netball girl. Nearly made the Sunshine Girls squad.'

'Sunshine Girls?' Rossi said. 'Who are they?'

'The Jamaican national netball team. My girl nearly made it.'

Delyse said uncomfortably, 'That's ancient history, dad.'

Eldon said to Rossi, 'Stay and watch the rest of the match. Have dinner with us.'

'Hold on,' Delyse said. 'I'm not cooking, especially for him.'

'Tell you what,' Rossi said. 'I noticed a fish and chip shop as we drove in. How about I treat us all to a fish supper?'

'I love fish and chips,' Eldon said, 'but we couldn't let you spend that sort of money on us.'

'My Chief Super has authorised hotel expenses overnight. I'll find somewhere cheap and the excess will pay for our tea. I offered Delyse to split the expenses if I could sleep on your sofa overnight.'

Delyse looked at her father, fully expecting his disapproval. To her surprise he said, 'That's a good idea.'

'Dad! You couldn't possibly condone his fiddling expenses like that.'

'It's called perks of the job, Delyse. Are you so well off you can refuse Clifton's generous offer?'

'It's immoral. Possibly illegal.'

'Don't be silly, Delyse. It's not like Clifton is taking bribes from criminals or deliberately fiddling the books.'

'It would save all that driving,' Rossi said. 'And we could set off for London much earlier.'

Delyse said, 'All right, but you're to sleep down here, not upstairs. All the facilities you need are downstairs.'

'Have you got a spare toothbrush?'

'Bloody hell, use your finger!' Delyse shouted.

'That's settled then,' Rossi said. He stood up and took his wallet from his back pocket. He took out a ten pound note and offered it to Delyse.

'I thought you were going to fetch the fish and chips,' Delyse said.

'I'm watching the cricket with Eldon. You don't mind popping out, do you?'

Delyse snatched the banknote and strode out to the hallway. Rossi followed and said, 'I'll have a saveloy with mine, please . . . Sunshine Girl.'

Delyse flipped him the finger, went out and slammed the front door.

'Aussies lost another wicket,' Eldon called out. 'LBW to an Edmonds spinner.'

8

At ten thirty the next morning, Rossi and Delyse arrived outside the embassy of the Soviet Union, Harrington House in Kensington Palace Gardens. They found, to their irritation, that the embassy did not open for visitor business until two p.m. They stood outside the ornate iron gates staring at the cream coloured mansion.

'What shall we do?' Delyse asked.

'It's a nice day,' Rossi replied. 'How about a stroll around Hyde Park and an early lunch. We only had toast for breakfast. Lunch will be my treat to make up for upsetting you last night.'

'A stroll sounds good,' Delyse agreed. They set off along Bayswater Road. 'You didn't upset me last night. You annoyed me.'

'Is there a difference?'

'Definitely. I have to admit you did my father a power of good. You two banging on about bloody cricket for hours annoyed me but cheered him up. He was wary of you at first.'

'Why? Another wicked white man?'

'Not that. He was worried about his little girl being taken advantage of.'

'Me, take advantage of you? I might as well try to take advantage of a steamroller.'

'Is that how you see me, steely, cold and hard?'

'Of course not. You're not a pushover, you know how to look after yourself. I respect that. I like your dad. He cares for you a lot. He loves you, wants the best for you.'

'I know,' Delyse sighed, 'but sometimes he tries to control everything I do, especially as I chose the same profession as him.'

They walked down Broad Walk and chose a bench overlooking the Round Pond to watch the swans and the ducks. A pleasant light breeze ruffled the reeds. The faraway noise of London traffic was like the echoes of a distant land.

Rossi asked. 'How long have you lived in England?'

'My mum and I moved here when I was sixteen. Dad was not best pleased to be abandoned in Jamaica but mum decided she needed a fresh start and we had family over here.'

'Do you still see your mum?'

'No, she died eight years ago. Cancer.'

'I'm so sorry. That must have been tough.'

'That was only the half of it. My marriage broke up. The rat bastard left me high and dry and homeless.'

'You've been married?'

'You needn't sound so surprised. Some people find me loveable.'

'I didn't mean to imply you were unloveable or unattractive. You're very attractive but you've never mentioned that you were once married.'

'We're partners but not bosom buddies. But thank you for the compliment.'

There was an awkward silence. To break the tension, Rossi said, 'I've no right or room to gloat about marriage break-up. My wife recently left me. Actually, I last saw her on the day we started this case. She's going to run a hotel in Bournemouth. Bournemouth? A town full of geriatrics is more exciting than living with me. How did your dad end up in Britain?'

'He took early retirement. Having been a Senior Super he had a tidy nest egg and a good pension. After mum died and my marriage broke up he came to England to look after me and bought that house so we both had a secure home. I owe him a great deal for that.'

'Even though you feel suffocated at times.'

'All the bloody time,' Delyse shuddered. 'Let's talk about something else.'

After lunch at the Serpentine bar they arrived back at the Soviet embassy just after two o'clock. They produced their warrant cards at reception and explained the purpose of their visit. The receptionist, a tough looking man who Rossi thought was certain to be KGB, said, 'I will ring Mrs Nikitina.'

'Is she a heavy smoker?' Rossi smiled.

The receptionist looked puzzled. 'I believe she smokes cigarettes but not heavily. I will call her.'

The receptionist found a colleague to show them to Mrs Nikitina's office. They went up in a lift to the second floor and were ushered into a large office space in which several people, mainly women, were working. Mrs Nikitina's office was at the end of the room, her private glass panelled domain. She was a tall, thin, almost gaunt woman, with garish dyed orange hair and inexpertly applied make-up. She did, however, exude an air of command and efficiency. She invited Delyse and Rossi to sit down and said, 'Now then, my dears, what can I do for you?'

Rossi was taken aback. He said, 'You speak very good English, Mrs Nikitina.'

'I have lived longer in England than I ever did in Russia, and I attended Oxford University. What did you expect, a grunting tractor driver?'

'No, I . . .'

'As I did not expect a British police officer to be a coloured woman. Are you really a detective sergeant, my dear?'

Mrs Nikitina said it so innocently and charmingly that Delyse was surprised to find she was not as offended as she should have been.

'Yes,' Delyse said, 'I am a "coloured" police officer. Now, shall we get down to business?' She took out a post mortem photograph of the hotel victim and handed it across the desk. 'This man was found dead in a hotel room and we are trying to establish his identity.' Delyse explained most of the salient circumstances except those agreed with Rossi should be held back or "adjusted".

'How intriguing,' Mrs Nikitina said. 'You say he was completely naked and somebody had stolen all his possessions.'

'That's correct,' Rossi said.

'Do you suspect he was murdered?'

'No,' Delyse lied. 'We think it was natural causes. The post mortem did not reveal anything suspicious.'

'Why do you think he is Russian or from another country of the USSR?'

Delyse took out a photograph of the spectacles with the eagle mark.

'Ahh, yes, the Opnah symbol. Only sold within the USSR and its satellite countries. Well discovered. I do not recognise this man but my girls out there have extensive files on Soviet personnel, including missing persons. I will see if we can identify this man and let you know.'

'Here are his fingerprints and dental records. Can we wait?' Delyse asked.

Nikitina pursed her pips. 'It may take two or three hours.'

'We would rather wait,' Rossi said.

Nikitina shrugged. 'Very well, I will search now.' She left her office and summoned one of her assistants. After a consultation they called in three more women. They searched seemingly endless files for over two hours. Nikitina returned and said, 'I'm sorry, we cannot identify this man. He is unknown to us. Please leave these photographs and your details and, if anything changes and we can identify him, we will let you know immediately.'

Rossi and Delyse left the embassy. Rossi said, 'Fancy a walk to King's Cross?'

'Are you crazy? We get the Tube. Or a taxi.'

'I haven't had my proper exercise today. Come one, it's not far. You enjoyed our stroll around Hyde Park.'

Delyse sighed. 'Okay. Trust me to get partnered with a keep fit fanatic.'

'That's the spirit,' Rossi said as they set off. 'The Russkis are a big disappointment. Where do we go from here?'

'I think the next step will be to circulate the photo and details of the victim to every force in Britain and see if anyone can recognise him.'

'Shall we give him a name?'

'How do you mean?'

'Instead of calling him the victim, or deceased or corpse, let's give him a name, you know, like John Doe.'

'How about Ivan Doe?'

'That's perfect, comrade.'

9

Rossi and Delyse arrived at King's Cross mainline station and found their train to Hertford North was leaving from Platform Nine in ten minutes. They walked alongside the line of grubby carriages. Second class was already crowded. At an empty first class carriage Rossi opened the door and started climbing in.

'Whoa, what are you doing?' Delyse asked angrily. 'That's first class.'

'Of course. I like to travel first class on trains. I like to be comfortable.'

'We've only got ordinary second class day return tickets.'

Rossi sighed with exasperation. 'Are you always this straight, Delyse?'

'Are you always this bent? What happens when the ticket inspector comes checking.'

'We outrank him. We are police officers in pursuit of a dangerous suspect and it was necessary to enter the first class carriage as part of our surveillance operation. We flash our warrant cards and Bob's your uncle.'

'Bob's your uncle visiting in prison after having been dismissed from the force you mean.'

'Come on, head prefect, the carriage is empty. No-one is going to care.'

Delyse reluctantly followed Rossi. They took two seats, facing each other, at a table on the left hand side. The seats were upholstered in royal blue, well-padded and furnished with arm rests. Delyse said sheepishly, 'I have to admit this is much more comfortable than the cattle trucks.'

Rossi laughed. 'Trust me to look after you, partner.'

After a couple of minutes Delyse said quietly, 'That's odd. Two men have entered the carriage but they're standing by the door instead of coming in.'

'Perhaps they prefer to stand. Hang on, there's two come on board the other end. They're just standing there as well.'

'Are they looking at us?'

'Yes, and they've stopped a couple of other people entering the carriage.'

The train slowly moved out of the station.

'They might be KGB,' Rossi said.

'So we're stuck on a train with ruthless Russian assassins,' Delyse said.

A tall heavy set middle-aged man came through from the adjoining carriage and was walking towards them. He said, 'Don't worry. They're not assassins. They're rather nice chaps actually, unless you get the wrong side of them. Mind if I sit down?'

The man did not wait for a reply as he sat down next to Rossi. He was wearing a light white raincoat over his suit even though the day was warm with no sign of rain. He had brown hair, only slightly thinning, with salt and pepper sideburns. His grey eyes twinkled with amusement and he smiled easily. He had heavy set jowls and a red veined nose which hinted at a drinking problem. Delyse guessed he looked older than he actually was. The man said, with a tone of authority, 'Identify yourselves, please.'

Delyse said, 'You first. We are police officers.'

'If that is true then you are obliged to show me your warrant cards before I answer any questions.'

Delyse hesitated then took out her warrant card, as did Rossi. The man examined both warrant cards and nodded thoughtfully. 'Detective sergeants from Bedfordshire and Hertfordshire working together. I'm intrigued.'

Delyse said, 'What makes you think we're working together?'

'It's a reasonable assumption from what we have observed. Your body language suggests you are not lovers. Or even friends.'

'Who are "we" and why have you been following us. You might find yourself arrested if you don't start talking.'

The man produced his own warrant card. 'I'm afraid you're rather seriously outranked. I am Commander Turnbull of Special Branch.'

Rossi checked the warrant card and said, 'What do you want with us?'

'You might be very useful to me in a little investigation I'm running. You visited the Soviet embassy today to try to establish the identity of the murder victim found in the Road Star Lodge.'

'Why do you think it was murder?' Delyse asked.

'I'm a commander in Special Branch, sergeant. That means I can poke about anywhere and get answers from pathologists, your superiors, or anywhere if it's a situation likely to affect national security, so don't try to play your detective interrogation tricks on me. I know everything, except the one thing we both want to know.'

'The identity of the victim?' Rossi suggested.

'Well done, bright boy,' Turnbull said. The train flashed through a station. 'Ah, Potters Bar already. I'd better hurry this along.'

'How did you know we had visited the embassy today?' Rossi asked.

'Mrs Nikitina, I should think,' Delyse said. 'She sounds more English than the English.'

Turnbull shrugged. 'Never mind how we know, that's above your pay grade. I'm going to show you a photograph taken at a recent garden party and I want you to tell me if you recognise anyone in it.' He took out two ten by eight inch photos from his inside raincoat pocket and handed one each to Rossi and Delyse.

Rossi scrutinised his copy and said, 'There is the Lord Lieutenant of Bedfordshire and her husband. I can't remember their names. I've seen her a couple of times at official events but I've never met her. And there, if I'm not mistaken, is our murder victim. What was he doing at a posh reception like that?'

'Good question, sergeant, one to which we would very much like the answer.'

'Then have you simply asked this Lord Lieutenant woman?' Delyse said.

'We would, sergeant, but we don't want anyone at this reception to know we are investigating the people who attended.'

'Why *are* you investigating them?' Rossi asked.

'Once again, that is above your pay grade, for the time being, but now that one of the attendees has been murdered it gives the police a perfect excuse to investigate the Lord Lieutenant, her guests and her staff. A couple of local plods like you are perfect for concealing the true nature of the investigation. No offence.'

'Local plod is better than most things I've been called,' Delyse said sourly.

'Bad choice of phrase,' Turnbull admitted. 'I apologise. The next step in your investigation must be based on this gathering in the photograph. I want you to obtain a full list of every guest and all staff involved in this garden party. You will, of course, report to your superiors as usual on the murder case, but you will also report your findings to me, and you *must not*, under any circumstances, tell your superiors, or anyone else, that Special Branch is involved. Is that clear?'

Rossi nodded. Delyse said nothing.

Turnbull said, 'If you recognise anyone else in this photograph, tell me now.'

Delyse said, 'No, I don't recognise anyone.' She handed back the photograph but Turnbull said, 'Keep it, but don't show it to anyone else. What about you, Sergeant Rossi?'

Rossi had recognised someone he knew well but decided he was not going to throw him to the ravenous wolves of Special Branch, or even the tender mercies of Delyse Joseph, until he had talked to him.

10

Clifton Rossi raised his knuckles, put them down, raised them again and then weakly knocked on Chief Superintendent Pritchard's office door. Pritchard shouted to come in. Rossi entered and closed the door. Pritchard was at his desk, almost hidden behind box files. A desk lamp augmented the evening light from a high window. Rossi had always thought the office was decidedly cramped for a Chief Superintendent but Pritchard did not seem to mind. Lack of vanity and egotism were two of Pritchard's virtues.

'Working late today, Clifton,' Pritchard said jovially. 'You must be angling for a promotion. Getting dark in here. Switch the fluorescent on and sit yourself down. Have you come to report that you've cracked our mysterious Road Star Lodge death case?'

Rossi flicked the switch and the fluorescent ceiling tube flickered into light. 'No, sir, but I have come to interrogate a suspect in the case.'

Pritchard was puzzled. 'Who do you mean?'

'You, sir.'

'Me?'

'I'm afraid so, sir. I've waited until most of my colleagues have gone home so they wouldn't see me enter your office.'

Pritchard's demeanour had changed from joviality to frowning concern. 'Sit down, boyo, sit down. Is this a joke, Clif?'

'Decidedly not, sir. First of all, let me say that I appreciate all you have done for me throughout my career and, especially in view of our exploits with the cricket team, hope we are friends as well as colleagues, despite the great

55

disparity in our respective ranks, and despite you lumbering me with Sergeant Joseph.'

'A nice speech but ominous. I consider you a friend, yes. And a good detective. How are you getting on with the black girl?'

Rossi felt an unexpected urge to defend the "black girl". 'Sergeant Joseph and I are warily circling each other, sir. She is a very good detective but understandably wary and defensive. She does not know I am interviewing you.'

'Well, get to the point. What am I supposed to do with the dead Russian?'

'We have not established beyond doubt that he was Russian but I'll get to that. Sir, it seemed peculiar you turned up at the Road Star Lodge early on that morning, in full uniform, to attend a common or garden suspicious death.'

Pritchard showed irritation. 'Nothing peculiar about it. I was on my way to work and heard the radio chatter. You know where I live. My route from home to work takes me right past the Road Star Lodge. I was intrigued by the circumstances and decided to pop in and have a look myself. I might be a Chief Superintendent but I'm still a working detective at heart and intrigued by unusual cases. Is that the only suspicion you have about me? Pretty thin I'd say.'

'If only it were, sir.' Rossi took out the Special Branch photo of the Lord Lieutenant's garden party and slid it across the desk.

'What's this?' Pritchard asked. He looked at the photo and, without hesitation, said, 'That's me there, talking with the Deputy Lord Lieutenant and several other invited guests.'

'What was the nature of this gathering? What was it for?'

'Nothing special. The Lord Lieutenant, as called for by her duty, holds regular gatherings of people high up in all

56

sorts of walks of life to thank them for their service and get a feel for what is going on in her county of Bedfordshire.'

'Including Russian gangsters?'

Pritchard threw down the photograph. 'What are you blathering about, Clif?'

Rossi leaned across and indicated with his forefinger. 'That is our dead Russian.'

Pritchard peered at the photo. He opened a desk drawer and took out a magnifying glass. 'Are you sure? It looks like him but it could be a coincidence.'

'It is definitely him, sir. Do you remember talking to him, or him to you?'

'No. As you can see, there were several people in attendance. I only spoke to a few of them and certainly not him.' Again Pritchard peered at the faces through the magnifying glass. 'Couldn't name any of them except the Lord Lieutenant and her husband. Wait a minute, where did you get this photograph?'

'I was wondering when you would ask that question. I've been warned in no uncertain terms not to tell you.'

'But I hope you're going to?'

'Yes. My loyalty is to you.'

'Who was it then?'

'Commander Turnbull of Special Branch.'

The colour drained from Pritchard's face. 'Special Branch!' he spluttered.

'He and his henchmen accosted Sergeant Joseph and myself on the train back from London. Special Branch had surveillance on the Lord Lieutenant's garden party, hence the photograph.'

'Then it's something political or diplomatic or international,' Pritchard said. 'I've heard of Turnbull. He is a powerful and influential figure in the police hierarchy. Did he give you any details?'

'No. He told us not to say anything to our superiors. He asked if we recognised anyone in the photo. I recognised you but I did not tell him. He doesn't know who you are.'

Pritchard sighed. 'It's just a matter of time before Special Branch investigate that reception.'

'They're not going to. We are. I mean Sergeant Joseph and I. Turnbull sees it as an ideal opportunity while investigating the murder of the Russian for us to investigate that garden party without the participants knowing.'

'How did Turnbull know it was the murdered Russian at the reception?'

'He said he has access to all the police and post mortem reports, and so on, but I strongly suspect he has an informant inside the Russian embassy.'

'Really? That wouldn't surprise me. What does surprise me is that Sergeant Joseph did not recognise me in this photograph.'

'She only met you for a few minutes and this is not your best side, sir. Will you give me your word of honour, as a senior officer and a friend, that your attendance at the same reception as the dead Russian is an entirely innocent coincidence?'

'I do give you my word, Clif. And I appreciate your respect for telling me. If Turnbull ever finds out you've grassed he'll have your balls for a handbag.'

'I'll take that risk. With your permission and approval I'll continue with the murder investigation and also the investigation into that reception.'

'Of course. Carry on, sergeant.'

Rossi stood up. 'I'll have that back, sir.' He picked up the photograph and left.

11

Delyse Joseph drove past Bedford Hospital and realised she had taken a wrong turn somewhere. She was intensely irritated by her mistake but much more irritated by Rossi's insistence on meeting her at his apartment rather than at the police station. He had refused to explain why.

After consulting her road map Delyse found the town centre and the river. She had to admit being enchanted by the view of the river as she drove over Bedford Bridge. She followed Rossi's directions and found his apartment building without further detours. She parked in an allotted visitor space, went in and took the elevator to the third floor. Primed and ready to go on the attack she knocked loudly on his door. The door opened ajar and Rossi peered out.

Delyse said, 'I hope you have a good reason for dragging me here like this?'

'I want you to see my flat,' Rossi said quietly.

'What's your game? You're not going to try anything stupid once you've lured me in?'

Rossi remained calm. 'Cricket's my game and as for luring you in, get over yourself. I simply want you to see where I live.'

'Okay, I'll get you a spread in *House Beautiful*. So let me in.'

Rossi held open the door and Delyse walked through into the small one-bedroom apartment. She looked at the ripped up carpets, the tipped over furniture, the opened drawers, the framed pictures torn off the wall and hurled on to the floor. She said, 'I love what you've done with the place but you've a lot to learn about feng shui.'

'That's why I asked you to come here.'

'I don't know anything about feng shui. What happened?'

'I came home from work last night and this is how I found it. The bedroom and kitchenette are in the same state. Whether it's simple vandalism or robbery, a warning, or someone was looking for something, we may have gotten ourselves involved in something more dangerous than we realised.'

'*We*,' Delyse repeated sarcastically. 'Why is this do with me? Perhaps it's revenge by some bad ass you've nicked in the past. Or perhaps your ex-wife was looking for your wallet. I bet it's well hidden.'

'I think they were looking for the photograph of the Lord Lieutenant's garden party.'

'Why do you think that?'

'Because my copy has gone. I left it in my bedside cabinet. Come and have a look.'

Delyse warily followed Rossi into his bedroom. It had been ransacked. On a wall mirror had been written, in lipstick: 'Leave it alone'.

Rossi said, 'Not my lipstick. The wrong shade. The threat is crystal clear. The perp stole the photograph and wrote that. Nothing else was taken. Whoever did this wants to make the reason so obvious that an imbecile would understand.'

'Lucky for you,' Delyse said. 'Special Branch gave us that photo. Could it be Commander Turnbull behind this?'

'Perhaps, if he was looking for something else, but I can't think what. It can't be the photo. He has a copy. So do you. Have you showed it to anyone?'

'No, no-one at all.'

'Not even your dad?'

'No, not even . . . oh, my God, perhaps they came to our house. Where's your phone.'

They rushed out to the living room. Rossi searched among a jumble of cushions and curtains, found the phone, plugged it back in and handed it to Delyse.

Delyse dialled. After a few seconds she said, 'Dad, are you okay?'

'Yes, of course,' Eldon said. 'Why are you asking? What is wrong?'

'Dad, have you had any visitors yesterday or today?'

'No. I've been here alone since you left for work. No, wait a minute, two men knocked the door yesterday. They claimed they worked for the gas board and a gas leak had been reported in the area. I asked them for identification but they didn't have any so I told them to bugger off. I dealt with many con men like them back in Jamaica. Think they can take advantage of an old man . . .'

'You did right,' Delyse said. 'I'm with Sergeant Rossi, Clifton. His flat has been ransacked. I'm not sure what is going on but we may have inadvertently got ourselves involved in a dangerous situation.'

'I'm intrigued,' Eldon said. 'Is there anything I can do?'

'Just be very careful and don't let anyone in the house, no matter who they say they are, unless you know them personally. Clif and I will investigate and soon get to the bottom of this.'

'Okay, darling. I'll be extra careful.'

Delyse put the phone down. 'They tried to get in my house but dad was too canny for them. That proves there must be a link to the case we are both working on. Who could it be? The Russians? Special Branch and that Commander Turnbull chap, but he has got the photograph and he knows everything we know. Nobody else knows about the photograph.'

Rossi sighed. 'Well, that's not strictly true.' He righted a dining chair and said, 'You'd better sit down.'

When Rossi finished explaining about Chief Superintendent Pritchard, Delyse exploded. 'After we were specifically ordered by Turnbull not to tell our superiors, you blab everything to Pritchard.'

'He's a good bloke. An honest copper. We're in the cricket team together.'

'Oh, well, that's it then! As long as he can bowl a googly and snick a run to offside he must be reliable.'

'So you do know your cricket after all?'

Delyse stood up and looked out of the window. 'I'll say this, you've got a great view of the river and the town. You'll enjoy the view going down when the KGB throw you out of the window.'

'That's why I bought this place, because of the view. I stretched my finances far beyond breaking point to buy it but I love it here. To see it trashed like this breaks my heart.'

Delyse looked around and sighed. 'I'll help you tidy up and then we can decide what we are going to do next.'

'That's kind of you but I can't expect you to help clear up this mess.'

'We're partners. For the time being. Besides, I think we've got a much bigger mess to clean up but I don't know where to start.'

'I do,' Rossi said vehemently. 'I apologise if I screwed up by blabbing to Pritchard. I say we do what our bosses ordered us to do and find out who our Ivan Doe is and who killed him. Everything seems to centre on this bloody reception held by the Lord Lieutenant. I suggest we confront this exalted ladyship and see what she has to say.'

12

Mallow Lodge came into view at the end of a long gravel driveway lined by mature silver birch trees. The verges were a thick riot of pink and purple mallow flowers. The lodge was a four storey Georgian building constructed with pale brown bricks. Windows and door frames were edged with white stone work. A set of white stone steps led up to a portico and a black front door.

Rossi parked the Lancia right in front of the house. 'Very nice place,' he commented to Delyse. 'Very posh. I'm glad your father made you dress appropriately in a sober suit. Grey suits you.'

'Father didn't make me, I chose this outfit myself. You're lucky. You have an easy choice, an entire rack of handmade Italian suits, sober or otherwise.'

'You're right there, partner. Saves having to think what to wear. Remind me what we know about the Latimers?'

'Family money on the husband's side,' Delyse replied. 'He was a colonel in the army until his retirement. His wife was in politics and was a Cabinet minister for a few years. Rich, well-connected, influential. That's how you get to be a Lord Lieutenant.'

'Something I'll never have to worry about.'

'Nor me. At least you're the right colour.'

They got out of the car, walked up the steps and rang the ornate brass doorbell. A young woman wearing a maid's uniform opened the door. They showed her their warrant cards.

'Oh, yes,' the maid said, in an east European accent. 'Please to come in and wait in the library. I tell Lord Lieutenant you are here.'

63

Delyse and Rossi were shown into a large well-lit room lined with books and furnished with a deep pile carpet and several well-padded armchairs.

The maid said, 'Please to sit down. May I bring you tea or coffee or other refreshments?'

They both refused refreshments and selected an armchair. After ten minutes a tall woman entered the library. Her hair was perfectly coiffed and she was dressed in the obligatory pearls and grey twinset with a black and white hounds tooth skirt. She was what used to be known as 'handsome'. Rossi stood up.

'Good afternoon officers, sorry to keep you waiting. I am Audrey Latimer. How can I help you?' She had the easy, slightly condescending manner of the socially superior; the easy gaiety that says "I'm superior to you but I'm a good sport and will pretend we are equals."

Delyse, feigning ignorance, said, 'We have actually come to see the Lord Lieutenant.'

The woman smiled and sat down. 'I am the Lord Lieutenant.'

'Oh. I expected the Lord Lieutenant to be a man.'

'And I didn't expect a police detective to be black. I wouldn't have expected you to be prejudiced, my dear, not someone from your ethnic background.'

Rossi saw Delyse bristling and made an unseen hand gesture for her to calm down. He said, 'We apologise. We were given to understand that you were a man.'

'Not very good detectives are you,' Mrs Latimer chuckled. 'How can I help you?'

Rossi said, 'It concerns a gathering that took place here on the evening of May 18th, a Saturday evening. Do you remember?'

'Yes, of course. It was one of the regular receptions we hold in order to meet people from all areas and strata of Bedfordshire society, as is my duty.'

Delyse said, 'Do you have a list of guests and staff and anyone else who attended this reception?'

'May I ask why?'

'It concerns an inquiry we are making into a possible criminal act. We assure you that you are in no way under suspicion.'

'Well, that's a relief!' Mrs Latimer chuckled lightly. She stood up and walked to a telephone on a side table. She explained, 'My husband, who is the Deputy Lord Lieutenant, arranged this function. He is working up in his office. I will call him.' She dialled a number and spoke to her husband. 'He'll be down in a couple of minutes. Have you been offered refreshments?'

'Yes, thank you,' Rossi said. 'We are fine.'

Mrs Latimer sat down. 'Well, this is exciting! May I ask the nature of the crime you are investigating?'

'Not at this point,' Rossi said.

Mrs Latimer turned to Delyse. 'Do you agree with your partner or are you both using the old good cop, bad cop routine?'

'We are not employing any "routine", Delyse said. 'Merely making general enquiries.'

'Of course. Where are you from, dear?'

'Hertfordshire CID.'

'No, I meant which country are you from?'

'I was brought up in Jamaica. And it's Sergeant Joseph.'

Mrs Latimer smiled sweetly and turned to Rossi. 'Do I take it you are one of the Italian contingent from Bedford?'

'If you like. My mother is English, my father Italian.'

'I think it's wonderful how immigrants are making such a contribution to English society.'

Rossi said, 'I am not an immigrant, I was born in England.'

'Quite, quite.'

The tense atmosphere was broken when the library door opened and in marched the Deputy Lord Lieutenant, Colonel Latimer. He carried a folder. He was an inch or two shorter than his wife. He was clean shaven, florid complexion, white hair thinning but neatly trimmed short. He was as erect and lean a figure as late middle age allowed and exuded confidence, good humour and bonhomie. His wife introduced Rossi and Joseph.

'Delighted to meet you both,' the Colonel said, shaking their hands. Delyse, despite her apprehension, felt she might like him.

'My wife tells me you need details of our little soiree here on May 18th?'

'Yes, sir,' Rossi said. 'Do you have a list of guests and any staff who were on duty that night?'

Colonel Latimer opened the folder and took out two sheets of paper. He handed one to Rossi and one to Delyse. 'That is a full list of guests together with their contact details.' He took out two more sheets of paper. 'That is a list of all the staff, including my wife and I. We generally use an outside catering firm for our bigger soirees. Everything you need is there.'

Delyse and Rossi studied the papers.

'This is very comprehensive,' Rossi said. 'Very helpful.'

'Glad to be of service,' the Colonel said. 'What is this all about? The soiree was all above board. You'll see that even your Chief Superintendent attended.' He laughed at the awkwardly lame alliteration.

Rossi nodded. 'I shall have to tread carefully.'

Both Latimers laughed politely at the feeble comment. The Colonel asked again, 'What is this all about? Can you tell us?'

Rossi looked at Delyse. She nodded in tacit agreement. Rossi took out a photograph from his jacket pocket. 'I would like you to look at this photograph and tell us whether you recognise this man. I have to warn you that the photograph was taken post mortem and is not very pleasant.'

The Colonel said, 'I was in the army, sergeant. I am sadly familiar with death and mutilation. Perhaps my wife does not need to see it.'

'Really, Hector, I am not the swooning maiden aunt you seem to think I am. If it helps solve a crime then it is my duty as Lord Lieutenant to look at the photograph.'

Rossi handed the photo to the Colonel. 'Was this man one of your guests?'

The Colonel studied the face. 'Yes, indeed,' he replied. 'He was here as the representative of a town in Czechoslovakia with which Bedford is twinned. I can't quite recall the name of the town. Audrey, can you remember?' He handed the photo to his wife.

'Pisek,' Mrs Latimer said. 'That's the name of the town. The Bedford-Pisek Twin Towns Association.'

'What was his name?' Delyse asked.

'Simonek. Yes, Radomir Simonek.'

Delyse looked at the guest list. 'Yes, there he is. It gives his address and phone number in Czechoslovakia.'

'That's right,' the Colonel said. 'He flew over especially for our little soiree. He was going to spend a couple of days here and then fly back. We offered to put him up here but he insisted on finding a hotel somewhere.'

'Had you met Mr Simonek before?' Rossi asked.

'No. I have been over to Pisek a couple of times to represent my wife and, of course, Bedford, but I had never met Mr Simonek before.'

Delyse asked, 'Did the Bedford-Pisek Town Twinning Association in Pisek send him over formally to attend your "soiree"?'

'No. Through our usual regular contacts they knew we were holding the soiree but we did not expect anyone to travel from Pisek to attend. We were delighted, weren't we dear?'

'Yes, delighted,' Mrs Latimer said, without enthusiasm. 'Sergeants, you say that this photograph was taken post mortem. Even as poor a detective as I can deduce it means Mr Simonek is dead. May I ask how he died?'

'He was found dead in his hotel room the morning after your reception,' Delyse said.

'Oh, goodness me. Natural causes, one assumes?'

'No, mam. He was murdered.'

Delyse carefully watched the reactions to her blunt statement. The Latimers seemed genuinely shocked.

Rossi asked, 'How was Mr Simonek behaving at the reception? Did he seem distressed or anxious? Was he drinking heavily or taking drugs?'

'Heavens no!' the Colonel exclaimed. 'We would not tolerate such behaviour. No, he seemed to be mixing affably. I talked to him for a while. He didn't seem to know much about Bedford, or Pisek for that matter, but said he had only lived there for a short time.'

They asked several more questions before Rossi said, 'You've been most helpful. We should leave you in peace. Sergeant Joseph, do you have any more questions?'

'No. We should get going.'

Colonel Latimer said to Rossi, 'Is that your car parked outside?'

'Yes, sir.'

'That's a very rare Lancia Delta Integrale, if I'm not mistaken.'

'That's right, sir. Not many people would recognise it. Are you a car buff, sir?'

'Indeed I am. I have a little collection of classic cars out in the stables if you would like to see them?'

'I'd love to.'

68

Delyse said pointedly, 'Don't you think we should get back and report?'

'It will only take a few minutes,' the Colonel said.

Mrs Latimer said, 'Please go and look at his little cars, sergeants. He has so few chances to show off.'

The Colonel laughed. 'That's true!'

13

Rossi and Delyse drove away from The Mallows and turned on to the narrow country road towards Bedford.

Delyse said, with an expression of disgust, 'That's twenty minutes of my life I won't get back, looking at a load of old cars.'

Rossi sighed. 'It was only ten minutes and I found it fascinating. It wasn't a "load" of cars, it was five.'

'Six, and more like twenty minutes. Still, if I had had to listen to the Colonel talking about his "little soiree" much longer I would have thrown myself under a car.'

'So you didn't like him?'

Delyse hesitated. 'Actually, he was all right. Bluff but likeable.'

'What about the Lord Lieutenant herself?'

'Supercilious, looking down her nose while trying to put on the common touch with a pair of plods.'

'She's aware of her exalted position but I thought she was all right.'

'That's because you grew up in the English class system. We who were brought up under the yoke of colonialism and white supremacy tend to bristle at the condescending upper classes.'

'The yoke of colonialism?' Rossi mocked. 'You were a little girl when Jamaica became independent!'

'The heel of the conqueror leaves a long and deep impression.'

Rossi snorted. 'What a lot of drivel. I didn't colonise Jamaica. Not my fault so why do I have to apologise.' He glanced at Delyse to find her smiling at him. 'Okay, nice one, you're winding me up. What did you think of the Latimers in relation to our case?'

'They didn't seem to be hiding anything or discomfited by our questioning. They provided the information readily, didn't appear to be dissembling. I'm sure that we'll find that Radomir Simonek is a false identity although why would anyone want to worm their way into the Deputy Lord Lieutenant's "little soiree" and then end up dead in a hotel room?'

'Good question. Two things struck me. Firstly, Colonel Latimer referred to "my" Chief Superintendent, that being Pritchard. How does he know that about me?'

'Okay, it's a thin theory but worth noting. What's the second thing?'

'Czechoslovakia is a tightly controlled Communist country and yet this Simanek character seemed to be able to travel easily to the UK at short notice.'

'Again, worth noting, but surely even the Communists don't object to town twinning agreements?'

'Anyway, I don't think the Latimers had anything to do with the murder. I agree they seemed to be dealing with us honestly. Perhaps they. . .'

'Don't you think you'd better slow down before this junction?'

Rossi was pumping the brake pedal. 'Shit, the brakes have gone. Hold on!' He snapped off the ignition and pulled up the handbrake. The Lancia veered violently left at the T junction. A bread van was coming towards them. Rossi wrenched the steering wheel to avoid the van. He saw a farm gate on the left. The Lancia was gradually slowing but Rossi had to get out of the way of oncoming traffic and aimed for the wooden gate. The gate smashed to pieces and they roared along a muddy track leading to a huge metal barn built on a concrete apron. Rossi pulled up the handbrake again. No effect. He wrenched the wheel as hard as he could. The Lancia slewed around, mud spraying everywhere, skidded on to the concrete apron and the rear end slammed into the barn.

Rossi and Delyse were shaking and breathing heavily.

Rossi asked, 'Are you hurt?'

'No.' Delyse said, 'You really know how to show a girl a good time.'

'You're welcome.'

'What happened?'

'The brakes failed, and someone helped them fail'

'What do you mean?'

'When brakes fail naturally by losing brake fluid its usually through a hole in a brake pipe or a loose fitting with enough fluid left to allow some braking power and you can feel it failing. These brakes failed without warning.'

'You think someone was trying to hurt us or kill us?'

Rossi didn't answer. They climbed out of the car. Delyse found her legs were weak and shaky. She held on to the car for support. Rossi inspected the smashed tail lights and caved in back wing. Then he ducked down. Delyse heard him scrabbling under the car. She said, 'What are you doing under there?'

Rossi, clothes streaked with mud, appeared and held up something. He said triumphantly, 'Brake pipe cut cleanly in half and held together with tape. It was bound to give way after a few pumps of the brake pedal.'

Delyse, strength returning, stepped back and inspected the car herself. 'It must have been done at the Latimers.'

'Yes, but why? Is it their doing? Are we being followed? Who was searching my apartment? Was it the Latimers, the Russians or has Commander Turnbull landed us in something bigger than we imagined?'

'All good questions,' Delyse agreed. 'By the way, you are filthy. And you smell, but that was a hell of a good piece of driving.'

14

Rossi said, 'Excuse me, do you mind if we sit here?'

Commander Turnbull looked up from his shepherd's pie with irritation. 'The pub is almost empty. There's plenty of room. Couldn't you . . . oh, it's you two.'

'We'll take that as a yes,' Rossi said. He and Delyse sat down at the small round table. Turnbull moved his pint and copy of the *Racing Post* to make room for his uninvited guest's drinks.

'Picked any winners?' Rossi asked, nodding at the *Racing Post.*

'Not in you two,' Turnbull said wearily. 'What are you doing here?'

'Interrupting your lunch,' Rossi said. He looked around. 'The *Prince of Wales.* I love these old Victorian London pubs. All stained glass and gleaming brass and polished wood.

'Why don't you stay here and admire the décor and see me in my office later?'

Delyse said, 'You might prefer some privacy and secrecy after what we have to say.'

'How did you know I'd be here?'

'You have your lunch here most days.'

'How did you know that? Have you been tailing me?'

Delyse ignored the question. 'I suppose you like to get away from the office to indulge your vices, such as gambling. And shepherd's pie.'

Turnbull folded up the *Racing Post* and put in it his jacket pocket. 'This conversation ends now. Come to headquarters if you want to see me. By the way, hadn't you better call me "sir"?' He made to stand up.

'Sit down, Commander,' Rossi said. 'We want answers before we respect your rank. You have got us involved in something much bigger and more dangerous than we anticipated.'

'What are you talking about? All you needed to do was obtain the guest list for that reception and identify the dead Russian in the hotel room. Have you done that?'

Delyse said, 'He attended the garden party as Radomir Simonek and claimed to be a member of the Bedford-Pisek Town Twinning Association from Pisek in Czechoslovakia. We checked. Pisek had never heard of Simonek. It's an alias.'

'Hmm, so no further forward. Did you obtain the guest list from the exalted Lord Lieutenant?'

'Yes we did,' Delyse said.

Turnbull held out his hand. 'Let me have it.'

'Not until you've answered a few more questions,' Rossi said.

'You do not have the rank to interrogate me,' Turnbull said angrily. 'Hand over the guest list or I'll have you two arrested for obstruction of justice.'

'That's not going to happen,' Delyse said.

'You cannot stop me. Hand over.'

'We think your wife might be interested in a certain flat in Battersea you visit on a regular basis. She and your three children will be very interested in certain services you obtain there, and your superiors will be very interested in the substances you obtain there. A little bit of ganja might be okay, but cocaine? That would be the end of your career, Commander.'

'You two bastards have been spying on me? I'll make it my business to fuck you both up. If you threaten my career, I'll ruin yours.'

'Like you nearly ruined our lives with your dirty tricks,' Rossi said.

'What are you talking about?'

'Someone cut the brake pipe on my car while we were interviewing the Lord Lieutenant and her husband. We were damn nearly killed on the way home.'

'That was not my doing. Not Special Branch.'

'Who else knew we were going to interview the Latimers?' Delyse said. 'You told us to keep it away from our superiors.'

Rossi said, 'Also my apartment was ransacked and two dubious characters attempted to gain entry to Sergeant Joseph's home.'

Delyse said, 'There must be a much more important reason why you are interested in the Lord Lieutenant's reception and the dead Russian. We want the whole truth. Do not try to manipulate us into doing your dirty work.'

Turnbull sat back and regarded the two detectives with distaste. 'Do you have the guest list here? If so, look on the list for another guest named Harry Falconer.'

Rossi took out the list and scanned for the name. 'Yes. His name is here. Do you want his address?'

Turnbull shook his head. 'It would undoubtedly be a false address or a front.'

'Who is Falconer?'

'He is a very clever and ruthless gangster, one of London's top villains. He is highly intelligent, cunning, never does his own dirty work but operates through a system of cut-outs. He owns a club where he and his henchmen meet, the Lucky Black Cat, a sort of rip-off of the Playboy Bunny clubs. We've been trying to pin something on him for years. He is under constant surveillance, that's how we knew he was at the Lord Lieutenant's party. I want to know what he was doing there.'

'Hold on,' Delyse said. 'Why was a London gangster invited to an event where the Lord Lieutenant meets people from Bedfordshire walks of life?'

'He was born in Luton but moved to London when he was a child. He donates to Luton charities but also has his slimy tentacles in Luton crime circles. He's probably conned the Latimers into believing he is a simple businessman.'

'If he is an ordinary criminal, however powerful, isn't it simply a police matter? Why are Special Branch involved?'

'Good question. We suspect Falconer is trying to set up links with other criminal factions, within London and outside. Some of these factions are linked with other countries. The Russian mafia, the Chinese Triads, and the Yardies from Jamaica, for instance. If all those factions started co-operating and working together it could be very serious for society. We need a way to get inside these criminal organisations but we need someone with links and inside knowledge, someone these gangs will trust.'

Rossi said, 'So you were thinking our dead Russian was making contact with Falconer in the seemingly innocent surroundings of the party?'

'That's right. But if we can't identify the Russian, we can't prove anything. We need a way to get near Falconer and infiltrating a rival gang with whom he is willing to co-operate and share the spoils is the best way. The Yardies would be ideal.'

'Why do you say that?' Delyse asked.

'Because the other gangs I mentioned, Russian Mafia and Triads, are more cohesive in their organisational structure and subject to control and commands from central organisations overseas. Falconer's cohorts are drawn from the south London underworld and are well-known to each other. Any attempt to infiltrate Falconer's gang itself is well-nigh impossible. The Yardies, on the other hand, are a group of separate gangs with no overall command. If we could infiltrate a powerful Yardie gang we might be able to get to Falconer through them if we could set up a mutually beneficial partnership. Trouble is, the Yardies are also tight knit and obviously suspicious of white people so we have not found a way to make contact with them.'

'Okay,' Rossi said. 'That all makes sense but who do you think is responsible for searching my apartment and cutting the brake pipes on my beloved Lancia?'

Turnbull shrugged. 'I don't know, sergeant, but I swear on my children's life it was not Special Branch. My search teams are so skilled that you would not even know they had been in your apartment. Sergeant Joseph, you look miles away.'

'Yes, Commander. You mentioned looking to find someone with knowledge of, and contacts within, the Yardies. I think I know just the man.'

15

Eldon and Delyse Joseph entered the cramped upstairs surveillance room to find Clifton Rossi and Commander Turnbull already in place.

Delyse said, 'Commander Turnbull, this is my father, retired Senior Superintendent Eldon Joseph of the Jamaican police service.'

The two men shook hands. Turnbull said, 'Welcome to the *Prince of Wales*. It's an honour to meet such a distinguished member of a brother police force, and I thank you for arranging this "encounter". I sincerely hope you have taken every precaution to protect your safety.'

'Don't worry about me,' Eldon replied. 'This man Falconer will know nothing of my involvement. My contacts with the Yardies have accepted the promise of immunity. They are as anxious to rid London of Falconer and his gang as you are.'

Turnbull said, 'I hope your Yardie contacts fully understand this is a temporary amnesty. Once Falconer is locked up the Yardies cannot expect *carte blanche* for their criminal activities, although we at Special Branch will no longer be involved. It will once again be a matter for the Metropolitan police.'

'They know the rules of this game, Commander.'

'Excellent,' Turnbull nodded. He turned to Delyse and Rossi. 'Your superiors have been told you've been seconded to assist in a Special Branch operation but they have not been told the nature of the operation. If all goes well I've no doubt a commendation will be added to your service records.'

Rossi said, 'Thank you, sir, but we have still not identified our dead Russian.'

Turnbull waved his hand in annoyance. 'Don't worry about that now. There's no evidence he was up to no good.'

Delyse said, 'With respect, sir, the dead Russian posed as someone called Radomir Simonek to infiltrate a gathering of some powerful and influential people. That suggests he was up to no good.'

'Yes, yes. You can follow that up after we have dealt with Falconer. Now, let me show you this equipment. This pub is sometimes used by Special Branch for such surveillance work so please do not disclose its location to anyone else, not police colleagues or family or anyone. Is that clear?'

'What does the landlord think of all this?' Rossi asked.

'He is a former officer in Special Branch who understands the need for a "facility" such as this.'

Delyse said, 'No wonder this is your regular haunt for lunch, Commander.'

Eldon said, 'I bet Special Branch gave him the money to buy this pub.'

'That is classified information,' Turnbull said, albeit with a smile. 'Now, take a seat. These two large screens show the games room below from two different angles. We'll be able to see and hear and record, with this tape machine, everything that goes on in that room. Criminals and gangsters prefer to meet each other in a public space and although this games room is separate its right next to the main bar but also gives privacy, or so they think. You can clearly see the snooker table, the dart board and the television for showing sports events and so on. The fervent hope is that Falconer and his cronies say enough to implicate themselves in their nefarious activities.'

'Isn't this called entrapment?' Delyse asked.

'You've been watching too many American police shows,' Turnbull said. 'We are not trapping anyone, merely recording whatever they say with this state-of-the-art equipment. Such evidence is permissible in British courts.'

'I share my partner's concerns,' Rossi said. 'How do you know the Yardies will keep their end of the bargain? Aren't they as ruthless as Falconer and his cronies.'

Before Turnbull could answer, Eldon said, 'The Yardies are certainly ruthless but it is a common misconception that they are one big criminal organisation. The Yardies are a loose collection of individual gangs, which makes them much easier to control than a cohesive criminal empire such as the Mafia or the one Falconer seeks to build.'

'Thank you, Eldon,' Turnbull nodded. 'I can tell our sergeants have grave reservations but what can go wrong? If we succeed in putting Falconer away, it will be a big gold star on your service records. If we fail it's not your fault at all. You will have done your duty.'

Rossi and Delyse looked at each other. Delyse said, 'When operations go wrong it tends to be the junior officers who are the scapegoats, especially if they are the wrong gender or ethnicity.'

'So cynical!' Turnbull grinned, in an attempt to change the subject. He looked at the screens as the video tape machine started whirring. 'Here we go. Look, first to arrive Falconer himself and a henchman. They are looking around for hidden traps or bugs.'

'Only two of them?' Rossi asked.

'Yes. Two of them and two representatives of the Yardies. That was the deal.'

'Falconer looks every inch the gangster,' Delyse said. 'Tall, thick greasy hair, sharp suit, eyes darting everywhere.'

'And as cunning as a fox,' Turnbull agreed.

The landlord entered the games room carrying a tray full of drinks. He set the drinks down on a side table and hastily withdrew. Several minutes passed with no sign of the Yardies.

Turnbull looked at Eldon. 'I hope your boys are not going to let us down.'

'They are not "my" boys. They will turn up late. It's a power trip thing.'

Another few minutes passed with Falconer and his henchman impatiently checking their watches. They were about to leave when the Yardies walked in. The two pairs eyed each other suspiciously.

'Here we go,' Turnbull said. 'Now to nail the bastard.'

No sooner had the discussion began when another two men entered the games room. All talking stopped as the six men watched each other warily. Falconer said, 'Who the fuck are you two?' He turned to the Yardies. 'The agreement was two representatives from each side. Who are they?'

'Nothing to do with us,' the Yardie leader said. 'We don't know who they are?'

Turnbull said agitatedly, 'I recognise them. They are Russian Mafia. What are they doing here? How did they know about this meeting?'

Three more men, Asian in appearance, entered the games room.

'They are Triads!' Turnbull exclaimed. 'This is insane! How did they know about this meeting?'

'Weapons are being drawn,' Rossi said. 'Hadn't you better go down and stop this?'

'No, they can't know we're up here and this is a set-up.'

'You better do something. Another pair of likely lads have turned up.'

Turnbull looked at the screen and groaned. 'They are IRA. We've had them under surveillance for months. Let me ring the landlord. They don't know he's ex-Special Branch. I'll tell him to ring the police.'

Turnbull left the room. The others continued watching the screens with horror. Pushing and shoving had turned into fisticuffs. Guns and knives were being drawn. The landlord appeared in the doorway aiming a shotgun. He shouted, 'The police have been called. Get out before they turn up and arrest the lot of you.'

There was a scramble to get out of the door and within seconds the games room was empty. Falconer was the last to leave, walking out coolly. The landlord put down the shotgun and, with a trembling hand, reached for a bottle of whisky and took several long gulps to soothe his nerves.

Commander Turnbull came back in the screen room, his face grim and angry. 'The whole meeting was betrayed and turned into a farce and I'm going to find out who did it. Eldon, you arranged for the Yardies to be here, did you let something slip or take a bribe.'

Eldon stood up angrily. 'No, I did exactly as you requested and to suggest I'd take a bribe is outrageous.'

Delyse stood up to defend her father. 'My father would never do anything so despicable. Nor would I.'

'What about you, Sergeant Rossi?' Turnbull asked. 'Did you betray this meeting?'

'Of course not, sir. But I know who'll get the blame for this fiasco.'

'Who?'

Rossi waved his hand at himself and the Josephs. 'We will. The lower orders, the lower ranks.'

'Especially with our skin colour,' Delyse said.

'Are you suggesting I would unfairly pin the blame on you?' Turnbull said.

'Yes,' Rossi said bluntly.

'I'll find out who did cause this cock-up, you can be certain of that.' Turnbull flounced out of the screen room.

'Well, that's our career down the pan,' Rossi said.

'How did we get mixed up in all this?' Delyse wondered. 'We were simply trying to identify Ivan Doe.'

'Special Branch will never trust me again,' Eldon said mournfully.

They heard sirens as police cars arrived outside the pub.

Rossi said, 'It's a good job the landlord intervened with his shotgun or else they would be dragging the bodies out.'

Delyse said, 'Perhaps we'll get another chance to nail Falconer and identify Ivan Doe.'

Rossi looked at Eldon and said: 'I love your daughter's optimism but I've a feeling we'll be blamed and taken off both cases.'

16

Chief Superintendent Pritchard looked across his desk at Clifton Rossi with a sour expression. He said, 'For God's sake, Clif! You've landed yourself, and me, in a handsome pile of manure. Is there anything you want to tell me before the others arrive?'

'No, sir. I'll say what I have to say in front of Sergeant Joseph and her boss. You've always treated me fairly and I'm truly sorry if the fall-out from this fiasco affects you, but I don't see why it should. You had nothing to do with it.'

Pritchard shook his head. 'That's the problem. I would have hoped you trusted me enough to report what you had got involved with, as you did when you found out I'd attended the Lord Lieutenant's garden party.'

Before Rossi could answer there was a perfunctory knock on the office door and Delyse entered, followed by Inspector Mallick. Introductions were made and Pritchard, as the senior officer, opened proceedings. 'First of all, I thank Inspector Mallick for travelling to Bedford station to attend this inquiry. It was ordered by our respective Deputy Chief Constables from Bedfordshire and Hertfordshire and is caused, and based on, this report we received from Commander Turnbull of Special Branch.' He held up a sheaf of papers. 'There is no need to go through the contents again. You two sergeants were there and Mr Mallick has studied the report. We, as your line managers, were under the impression that you two were investigating the death and identity of the dead Russian when, in fact, you had got involved in a scheme to bring down a top London gangster. I would have thought and hoped, and I'm sure Mr Mallick will agree, that you should have warned us what you were doing, even if you could not give full details.'

Rossi said, 'We were ordered, in no uncertain terms, by Commander Turnbull that we must say nothing to anyone about the Falconer operation.'

'Of course I understand that but I'm still disappointed you said nothing.'

'Turnbull is a Commander, sir. He outranks you. We were obeying the chain of command.'

'There is such a thing as personal loyalty. Wouldn't you agree, Inspector?'

'Certainly,' Mallick replied. 'I am disappointed that Sergeant Joseph did not see fit to warn me of this ill-judged operation. I have always tried to give her my support, being aware of the particular problems she faces within the force.'

'By "particular problems" you mean my colour?' Delyse asked wryly.

'Yes, and your gender.'

'I don't need special help.'

'Nevertheless I felt obliged to provide it. You are an excellent detective but that's not necessarily enough to thrive, or even survive, in a racist and sexist culture. Somebody should be on your side.'

Delyse nodded. 'You've always been fair to me, and I thank you, but, as Sergeant Rossi has pointed out, we were specifically ordered not to tell our superiors, or anyone, about the Falconer operation.'

'That's not strictly true, is it?' Mallick said.

'What do you mean, sir?

'I mean that you got your own father, Eldon Joseph, involved in this operation. A civilian.'

'Also a retired Senior Superintendent in the Jamaican police service. He volunteered his services because of his knowledge and contacts within the Yardie gangs. Without

85

my father there would have been no operation. Turnbull did not have the contacts.'

Pritchard said, 'I agree with Mr Mallick. Your father's involvement was most irregular, foolhardy and dangerous.'

'My father can look after himself.'

Sensing Delyse's growing agitation, Rossi intervened. 'Sir, the operation would have succeeded but someone betrayed us by tipping off other criminal elements who turned up at the same time. It was a clever ruse to destroy the operation.'

'Any idea who betrayed you?' Pritchard asked.

'No, sir. There were a few officers within Special Branch who helped set up the operation but Commander Turnbull vouches for their loyalty.'

Pritchard looked at Delyse. 'Perhaps your father's contacts in the Yardies were a little too cosy.'

This time Rossi could not hold Delyse back. She said, 'If you are inferring that my father is a traitor then I take great offence.'

Rossi stepped in. 'That makes no sense because the Yardies were set to benefit greatly by bringing down Falconer and his gang. Why would Eldon betray the operation he was instrumental in setting up? He had nothing to gain by such a betrayal.'

'He should not have been involved,' Mallick said.

There was silence for a few moments while tempers cooled.

Pritchard was conciliatory. 'Let's not keep going round in circles with pointless accusations. There is the question of disciplinary action.'

'For doing our duty as ordered by a senior officer in Special Branch?' Delyse said with astonishment.

'I told you we would be made the scapegoats,' Rossi added.

Pritchard help up his hands. 'Steady on,' he said. 'I suggest a report be added to your respective personnel files making it clear you followed orders but that it would have been wiser and more courteous to inform your superior officers of what you were doing. No blame will be attached to either of you for the failure of the Falconer operation. Chief Inspector Mallick, would you agree with that proposal?'

'Yes, sir. A fair resolution.'

Delyse said, 'So we can go back to investigating the dead Russian?'

'No,' Mallick said. 'Mr Pritchard and I agree that this cross-border co-operation experiment has not been successful. The dead Russian case will be handed over to a new team from Bedfordshire CID.'

Delyse said, 'Sir, I must protest. We have made good progress on that case and nearly been killed in the process. We must be allowed to carry on.'

Rossi said, 'I agree with Sergeant Joseph. This is our case. A new team will take days to get up to speed. I formally request permission to carry on investigating with Sergeant Joseph. I think we make a good team.'

Pritchard stood up. 'Request denied. Inspector, will you join me while I report to my DCC.'

'Certainly, sir.' He turned to Delyse. 'You wait here with Sergeant Rossi. Say your goodbyes. I'll be back in a few minutes then we'll return to Hertford.'

Pritchard grinned. 'My office isn't bugged. You can say what you like behind our backs.'

The two senior officers walked out.

Rossi stood up and looked out of the window. He said, 'I don't care what assurances they give, I'll bet a lot of the blame for the Falconer operation will attach to us.'

'I think you're right, and I'm more disappointed to be taken off the Ivan Doe case.'

Rossi nodded. 'It's almost like a cover up. We were close to cracking it. I can feel it in my bones.'

'There's something more going on.'

'What do you mean?'

'I still think it's a highly suspicious coincidence that the dead Russian, the gangster Falconer and your Chief Super Pritchard were at the Lord Lieutenant's "soiree" and now we've been taken off the case by the same Chief Super.'

'You're right but what can we do? If we go behind their backs again our careers will be in the mangle.'

'Umm,' Delyse said. 'Did you mean what you said, about us making a good team?'

'No,' Rossi smiled. 'I think we make a great team.'

17

Clifton Rossi was at his desk in the Bedford police station squad room. He looked up to see Detective Sergeant Don Murray approaching. Rossi broached himself to remain calm and get rid of the overweight, overconfident, overbearing Scottish prick as quickly as possible.

Murray leaned on Rossi's desk and said, 'Afternoon, consigliere.'

Rossi tried not to rise to the bait but could not help himself. 'Enough with the Godfather jokes. I don't call you Jock. My name is Clifton.'

Murray stepped back and held up his hands in mock alarm. 'Whoa, watch that dago temper!'

'I'm as British as you are, Don. What do you want?'

'Any progress on that post office hold-up?'

'Not much. I'm still waiting for the forensics report. I've made a few enquiries but there may be a new firm operating in the town.'

Murray frowned. 'Is that all you've got? Pritchard is not going to be pleased with you.'

'I can't help that. I'm doing what I can.'

A sly grin creased Murray's face. 'You haven't got that delicious black tart helping you now.'

'Don't call her a tart. She's a detective sergeant, like you.'

'I bet you had fun working with her. Did you two get it on?'

'No, we didn't. I had too much respect to try anything like that. It was purely a working relationship.'

'You're too slow, my Mafia friend. Everyone knows black girls are easy.'

'Don't talk racist rubbish, Don. She's a dedicated officer.'

'I've struck a nerve here,' Murray laughed. 'With any luck I'll get partnered with her and then I can try it on.'

Rossi snapped. 'Shut your filthy mouth.'

'What will you do? Have me whacked by your pals in the Mob.'

Rossi stood up, grabbed Murray by his necktie and pulled his face closer. 'I'm sick to death of your puerile Mafia jokes and even more sick of you making filthy innuendos about a fellow officer.'

Murray grabbed Rossi's hand and tried to pull away. 'Let me go, you mad bastard,' he shouted. 'It's only a bit of banter between the lads.'

A voice said loudly, 'What's going on here? You two, my office. Now!'

Rossi and Murray meekly followed Chief Superintendent Pritchard into his office.

Pritchard said angrily, 'Two of my officers openly fighting in the squad room? What was that all about?'

Before Murray could speak, Rossi said, 'It was my fault, sir. I over-reacted to a joke.'

'What was the joke?'

'A comment about somewhat I respect, sir.'

'What comment?'

'I'd rather not say, sir.'

Pritchard turned to Murray. 'Is that what happened?'

'Yes, sir. My joke was . . . misjudged.'

'Was the joke about me? I know I get called Taffy, and a lot worse, because of my Welsh ancestry.'

'Absolutely not, sir,' Murray said.

'It was not about you, sir,' Rossi confirmed.

Pritchard nodded. 'Okay, you're protecting each other and I respect that but don't let this happen again. Now piss off and get on with your work.'

Rossi and Murray left Pritchard's office. They parted without another word.

Rossi sat down at his desk and tried to analyse what had just happened. Murray was irritating but he was honest and harmless and a good reliable detective and Rossi was usually able to ignore his behaviour. What had struck a nerve this time? Deep down he knew but he thrust the notion back into his subconscious.

Two hours later the notion erupted into clear view when his telephone rang. He picked up and said: 'CID, Sergeant Rossi speaking.'

The voice was familiar and anxious. 'Clifton? It's Eldon. It's about Delyse. She's disappeared.'

'Disappeared? How?'

'She's taken a few days leave but she hasn't come home for the past two nights. She's not been seen at the station. Nobody knows where she is. She hasn't rung me or anything. She's seemed a bit down since you two stopped working together.'

'Did she say anything about where she was going or what she intended to do?'

'Not really but she did mention the other day that she was determined to find something on that Falconer chap. I've got a horrible fear she might have got herself into something too deep.'

'Try not to worry, Eldon. I'm coming to see you right away.'

18

Clifton Rossi walked towards the entrance of the Lucky Black Cat club. Hidden by the evening shadows he had been observing the entrance from across the road for over an hour. The entrance was surprisingly low key. Mahogany double doors under a discreet canvas canopy with subdued fluorescent strip lighting to highlight the doors. The bouncer was smartly dressed in a dinner suit with a Lucky Black Cat badge embellished with diamante on his lapel. Rossi crossed the road and walked unsteadily but confidently towards the doorman. Pretending to be slightly tipsy, Rossi said, 'Good evening.'

'Good evening, sir. Are you a member?'

'I certainly am,' Rossi answered.

The bouncer nodded and, without another word, opened the door.

Rossi found himself in a long, narrow foyer branching left and right, again illuminated by strip lighting and decorated by rows of silhouette pictures of young women wearing the Lucky Black Cat house costumes. At the right-hand end of the foyer was another pair of double doors. In front of the doors was a desk with another fit-looking bouncer sitting on duty.

'Good evening, sir,' said the bouncer. 'May I see your membership card?'

'I'm afraid I've left it at home,' Rossi said, pretending to sway slightly. He took out his wallet from an inside pocket and took out a £20 note. 'Is this acceptable?'

The bouncer stared at the note and said, 'I'm afraid that's no longer valid.'

Rossi took out another £20 note. 'How about two of them?'

The bouncer smiled. 'You really want to get in badly.'

'I feel lucky tonight. I want to give your casino a hammering.'

'I'm sorry, sir.'

'I'm a personal friend of Mr Falconer. Is he in tonight?'

The bouncer stood up. He was well over six feet tall. Rossi feared he was about to be ejected but the bouncer said, 'I'll have to pat you down for concealed weapons.' Rossi held his arms out while the bouncer searched his clothes and body. 'One more and you're in.'

Rossi pretended drunken insouciance. 'I'm gonna win it back anyway'. He handed over a third £20 note.

'Have a nice evening, sir.'

Rossi went into the club. He was surprised at how spacious it was. The ceiling was decorated with a huge cartwheel of light bulbs. To the right was a long padded bar, the full length of the room. Tables, chairs and sofas were arranged on different levels. On the left was the entrance to the casino with patrons moving in and out all the time. The club was busier than Rossi had expected, almost crowded. He threaded his way through to the bar and ordered a double Scotch on the rocks. Perched on a stool he surveyed the room without being too obvious. Right at the back was a table with three men, one of whom Rossi thought was Falconer, although the light was too dim to be sure. He had not come to confront Falconer.

After a quarter of an hour Rossi saw what he had come to find and was as shocked and surprised as he had ever been in his life. Delyse noticed him at the same instant. She momentarily hesitated then approached him. She was carrying a silver tray and was dressed, or rather undressed, in full Lucky Black Cat costume, high cut black and pink basque, black fish net tights, high heels, false tail and cat ears. She whispered angrily, 'What are you doing here?'

'Oh, nothing much, Delyse. Just wondering why my former partner has chosen a new career as a servile tart rather than as a good police officer.'

'Keep your voice down. That's Falconer sitting back there. If he finds out we're coppers we'll be in big trouble.'

'No shit, Sherlock. Are you working for him now?'

'Let me take this drinks order first.' Delyse ordered a round from the bar staff and took the tray into the casino.

Rossi was fuming angry but desperately worried. In a few minutes Delyse returned. Rossi said urgently,

'Whatever you are up to, it must stop now. You're in grave danger.'

'I'm undercover, you ass.'

'Unauthorised undercover. Your colleagues know nothing about your whereabouts and your father is worried sick.'

Delyse flinched at mention of her father. 'It's a private undercover job.'

'Oh, well, that's fine then. Perhaps Falconer won't slit your throat if you tell him it's a private job.'

'I couldn't leave it alone,' Delyse whispered. 'After having to abandon the Ivan Doe case and then seeing Falconer wriggling out of the sting we arranged, I had to do something.'

'I feel the same,' Rossi hissed, 'but this isn't the way to do it. Listen, you must get out of this place, now.'

'I can't. I have to . . .'

'No, Delyse. You must get out now. Is there a back way you can leave by?'

'Well, yes, but I'd have to collect my stuff first.'

'Leave your stuff and buy new when you're safe. I'm parked in Roscommon Street, a couple of streets along.'

'But I . . .'

'But nothing. If you don't leave now I'll arrange a police raid and get you out.'

'You're not my boss or my father. You can't order me around.'

'I can when you're placing yourself in a situation that, one way or another, could ruin your life. I swear we will go after Falconer and whoever killed the Russian but we'll do it with good old fashioned police work.'

'You mean that?'

Rossi could see the tension leave Delyse's face. 'Of course I mean it. We're a great team. I'll meet you at the car, however long it takes, just get away from here. Agreed?'

Delyse nodded and walked away. Rossi could not resist taking a last look.

19

'Slow down, for Christ's sake!' Delyse shouted.

Rossi realised they were roaring through the streets of London at a dangerous speed and took his foot off the accelerator.

'What's gotten into you?' Delyse demanded.

'Gotten into *me*?' Rossi repeated sarcastically. 'What's gotten into *you*? I haven't seen you for weeks then your father rings me, incredibly worried about your whereabouts, and I find you dressed as the worst kind of tart in a club owned by a psychopathic gangster and being ogled by all sorts of sweaty drunken oafs. What were you thinking?'

Delyse pulled the overcoat tight around her as she remembered how she was dressed. 'You know what I was thinking. We failed to find the identity of Ivan Doe and we've caught some blame for the abortive attempt to entrap Falconer. I thought if I could find evidence against Falconer it would offset the damage caused by those fiascos.'

Rossi slowed the car, pulled over to park at the kerb and switched off the ignition. He opened his door.

'Where are you going?'

'To that phone kiosk over there, to tell your dad that you're okay and will be home soon.'

Delyse said, 'No, wait a minute . . .', but Rossi was gone.

Minutes later Rossi came back and re-started the car.

'What did you tell my dad?' Delyse asked.

Rossi engaged gear and they set off. 'I told him you had been roped into a last minute surveillance job and you weren't able to contact him until now. I apologised for you.'

'You should apologise to me.'

'Why? For saving you from yourself? How on earth did you end up working in that ridiculous outfit?'

'I went into the club simply to see what it was like, what the layout was like, if it was worth putting surveillance on it. The bar manager immediately offered me a job as a cocktail waitress. After all, they would not suspect a black girl like me would be a copper. He said I would fit perfectly into the ethos of the Lucky Black Cat. He said I was tall with a good figure and great legs.'

'He's not wrong there.'

'I saw the chance, accepted and said I could work late and I was offered the use of one of the upstairs rooms to sleep so I didn't have to travel home.'

'Anything could have happened to you.'

'I can look after myself. I . . .'

'And what do you know about being a cocktail waitress?'

'More than you'd think. I worked as a waitress in Jamaica to help with my netball expenses. I was underage but I looked old enough.'

Rossi shook his head. 'And you were criticising my moral boundaries for fiddling expenses. I still don't understand what you thought you'd achieve with this stunt?'

'More than you think. I soon found out Falconer and his cronies used the small stock room at the back of the club for their most secret meetings. So I bugged the place.'

Rossi nearly choked. 'What?' he spluttered. 'How?'

'I had to use the stock room occasionally to fetch glasses or bottles, there was a telephone in there, so I bugged it with a voice activated tape recorder.'

'Did it pick up anything?'

'I don't know. I haven't had a chance to listen to the recording yet.'

'Then what are we waiting for. There's a Wimpy ahead. Are you hungry?'

'Starving'.

They found a table as far away from other customers as possible. Rossi ordered two burgers and two coffees and brought them to the table. Delyse took out the recording device, a miniature tape recorder, and placed it on the table. Delyse took a bite of burger and pressed play. They listened carefully but for minutes there was no sound except a faint hiss and an occasional sound of a door opening or bottles clinking. After fifteen minutes, which equated to several hours of potential listening time, there was nothing useful. Then they heard a door click shut and someone lifted the telephone handset and dialled a number.

Delyse and Rossi sat tense, watchful for other people overhearing. A voice said, 'We've made progress. Found a secure venue for the sex.'

Delyse paused the tape. 'That's Falconer's voice. Did he say sex?'

'That's what it sounded like to me.'

Delyse pressed play. The voice at the other end of the phone said, 'That's good news. What have you got?'

Falconer replied, 'It's an old abandoned pub called the Railway Tavern. It'll be good enough for the sex until we're ready to move. Any news when that will be from your end?'

'Not yet but I should have more details by the time of our next soiree.'

'Good. Be careful who you invite next time.'

The handset was replaced. Delyse and Rossi stared at each other. Delyse said, 'We know that voice. What affected upper class prick calls a garden party a "soiree"?'

'Indeed we do know. The Deputy Lord Lieutenant of Bedfordshire. You've found a definite link between him and the biggest gangster in London.'

Delyse smiled. 'Not so idiotic now, am I?'

'Okay. You've found a major breakthrough. Let's listen to the rest of the tape.'

They listened until the tape clicked off but there was nothing else except hissing and clinking.

'Umm, pity there's no more,' Rossi said, 'but we've established several things, Falconer and the Deputy Lord Lieutenant are in contact, their plan is something about sex, and a venue called the Railway Tavern is involved. What do we do know?'

'Did you say "we've" established these things?' Delyse said tartly.

Rossi held his hands up. 'You did it, I fully admit that. Are we going to our superiors with this?'

'No, they'll want to know where this information came from, and with all the leaks and blabbermouths in the force, word could get out to Falconer and the DLL that we're on to them. I suggest we investigate this ourselves. Finding a deserted Railway Tavern will be easy, wherever it is. We could put in a request to the local plod to keep an eye on that place and report back when activity starts. We can investigate the DLL from our end, in our spare time if necessary. What do you say?'

'I'm in. I want to nail these bastards. The references to sex suggest they may be importing girls from Russia or eastern Europe for prostitution, hence the presence of our Ivan Doe.'

Delyse nodded. 'We've got to stop them if they're exploiting women.'

'Ironic words from a women dressed as a sexy cat under that overcoat.'

Delyse threw her remaining burger at his head.

99

20

Two weeks later, at six thirty in the evening, Delyse and Rossi were sitting in the Lancia. It was parked in the entrance to a farmer's field nearly opposite the gated driveway entry to The Mallows.

Delyse picked up the thermos flask from the back seat. 'Would you like another coffee?'

'Yes, please,' Rossi said. 'You make good coffee.'

Delyse smiled. 'Jamaican Blue Mountain. Never mind that Brazilian stuff.'

'Anymore of those patties left? They're delicious. Did you make them?'

'Of course. Any good Jamaican girl is taught how to make our favourite snack.'

'I didn't figure you as domesticated,' Rossi smiled.

'I had to get domesticated. My mother taught me a lot before she decided she had tired of life with dad and me. Dad looked after me at first and gradually, as I grew up, I looked after him until we moved to England.'

'What about your marriage? What happened there?'

At first Delyse did not reply and Rossi thought he had over stepped the bounds. Then she said, 'I guess he wanted a domesticated and dutiful wife. That's not what I could give him. I was too committed to my career.'

'You loved him though?'

'Yes. I thought I did. I thought he loved me but he also had other commitments, mainly to booze and the floozy who worked as his secretary.'

'Was he white?'

'Why do you want to know that?' Delyse asked angrily. 'I don't ask you if your ex-wife was black!' Then, after a few seconds. 'Yes, he was white. Perhaps he saw me as his slave.'

Rossi was very uncomfortable. 'I'm sorry I asked. Did it sour your view of white men?'

Delyse shrugged. 'I'm not that prejudiced or shallow. He took everything I had but not all white men are the same. You seem decent enough.'

Rossi looked at Delyse. 'Steady on, sergeant. You almost paid me a compliment. You don't know what I was like in my marriage.'

'Okay, what were you like?'

Rossi's turn to hesitate. 'I loved Jane dearly, and I'm certain she loved me. And still does.'

'So why have you split up?'

'Partly the job. You know how difficult it is being the wife or husband of a copper when the other person isn't a copper, but we were getting through that. Then something happened that I couldn't deal with like a grown up, so I took to drink.'

Delyse waited but Rossi said no more. She said: 'Aren't you going to tell me what happened?'

'No. It's too painful.'

'I understand, but I'm your partner. I won't judge. Did you fall in love with someone else?'

'No, no. I was always faithful to Jane. Truly. What happened was nearly eight thousand miles away.'

Delyse considered this statement and asked, 'Do you mean the Falklands War?'

Rossi nodded reluctantly. 'My older brother was a sergeant in the Parachute Regiment. He was killed at the battle of Goose Green. I looked up to him, he was my hero, so much courage, good humour and kindness. His death broke our family. My parents have not fully recovered, probably never will, and neither have I. I took to the bottle to dull the pain. I've gotten over that, largely, but I doubt if I'll ever be the same again.'

'I appreciate your telling me. It explains a lot about you.'

'He wrote to me and, despite the fact they were trying to kill each other, he expressed sympathy for the Argentinian soldiers. Young and not properly trained he said. They were as terrified and reluctant to be mixed up in a war as the British lads. To kill each other because of a difference in nationality or belief or skin colour, or especially because some mad tyrant wants more power, is simply insane. He taught me much and I'm very proud of him.'

'I'm sure your brother would be proud of what you're doing, chasing the bad guys. You're a good copper, and your idea of hiding a surveillance camera in the Latimer's driveway was inspired.'

'Thanks. As we discussed, we cannot trust our superiors and it would have been impossible for the two of us to spare the time for this sort of surveillance full time.'

Delyse said, 'So come on, are you ever going to tell me from where you obtained that cine camera and where you analysed the film?'

'Let's just say I had to pay the Piper.'

Delyse was baffled. 'What does that mean? You don't mean Miss Piper from the Road Star Lodge?'

'As you so willingly pointed out, she was obviously smitten by my manly charms and I remembered her telling us she had an uncle who was in the surveillance business. After dinner and drinks she was only too willing to co-operate with the law.'

'Just dinner and drinks?'

Rossi laughed. 'You're not jealous, are you partner?'

'Jealous? No way, just wondering what other morally dubious situation you might have landed us in.'

'It was just dinner and drinks. Nothing morally dubious.'

'Are you going to keep seeing her?'

'When I return the cine camera, yes. After that, maybe not.'

Delyse punched him on the arm. 'Typical bloke, get what you want and then disappear.'

'We didn't get all that we wanted. After watching the tapes we haven't spotted any suspicious visitors or comings and goings except that Colonel Latimer goes out at the same time every Thursday. Now we can see what he gets up to.'

'Headlights,' Delyse announced. 'Yup, that's his Jaguar. Let's tail this entitled two-faced upper class sucker and find out where he goes.'

21

Rossi and Delyse followed Latimer's Jaguar until it entered the northern suburbs of Harlow New Town and stopped in a quiet residential street of run down 1960s council houses. Latimer got out and started walking. Rossi hastily got out and followed him at a discreet distance. After turning into another side road, Latimer stopped at a small, plain and undistinguished bungalow with attached garage which looked out of place among the semi-detached properties all around. Rossi concealed himself in the shadows as Latimer rang the front door bell and was quickly admitted.

Rossi went back to the Lancia and drove to where they could park and observe the bungalow, which had a small front garden guarded by tall hedges.

'Did you see who answered the door?' Delyse asked.

'No. Too dark,' Rossi replied. 'Couldn't even tell if the person was male or female.'

'Go and have a closer look.'

'What do you mean?'

'I mean go and look around the bungalow,' Delyse said impatiently. 'See if there are any curtains open where you can peek in. See who's in there and what's going on.'

'What if someone catches me?'

'Oh, for Christ's sake, you're a police officer in pursuit of a suspect in a criminal investigation! Are you a man or a wuss?'

'Why don't you go? We're in Hertfordshire. You're a Hertfordshire officer. I'm Bedfordshire.'

Delyse grabbed the door handle. 'What a gentleman! I'll go.'

'No, no. I'll do it.'

Delyse sighed as she watched Rossi suspiciously tip-toeing towards the bungalow. Rossi disappeared behind the bungalow. He returned to the car less than five minutes later.

'That was quick,' Delyse said, as Rossi climbed back in the car.

'Nothing to see,' Rossi replied. 'Curtains and blinds all drawn with no gaps anywhere. All we can do is wait.'

Two hours later Delyse was shaken awake. She had been sleeping on Rossi's shoulder.

'Uh, sorry,' Delyse said. 'I dropped off.'

'Latimer is leaving. Let's wait a few minutes to make sure he's clear and then go in.'

'Okay,' Delyse said, trying to clear the sleep from her head.

A few minutes later Rossi and Delyse got out of the car. 'Is this wise?' Delyse asked.

'What do you mean?'

'Latimer is in contact with Falconer. What if there are gangsters in that bungalow. Armed gangsters.'

'If we show our warrant cards when the door is opened we should be safe. For criminals to gun down two unarmed coppers would land them in a world of trouble.'

'That won't be much consolation when we're dead.'

'Come on, partner. Perhaps Latimer was visiting a friend or relative. You're expecting the worst.'

'I'm a black woman living in a white world. I usually find the worst.'

They walked up to the front door, warrant cards in hand. Rossi rang the bell. After several seconds there was no answer. Rossi rang again, knocked loudly and shouted through the letter box, 'Police officers! Open up!'

'That's a good idea,' Delyse said. 'Tell them we're coppers first so they can shoot us as soon as the door opens!'

Rossi tut-tutted impatiently. He rang and knocked loudly and repeatedly. Eventually the front door opened and, standing in a well-lit hallway, was a tall, voluptuous woman. Her long chestnut hair fell in waves down her back. She was strikingly beautiful. Her robe was undone. She was wearing a lacy black and red basque underneath. She was unfazed as Rossi and Delyse held up their warrant cards. She said, in an eastern European accent, 'No need to knock my focking door down. What do you want?'

Delyse said, 'We are conducting a criminal investigation and we want to question you about your last visitor.'

'Why?'

Delyse ignored the question. 'What was the purpose of his visit? And who are you?'

'Do you have a warrant?'

'No.'

The woman said, 'Then I can answer easily. Fock off and fock off.'

Rossi said, 'In that case we will have to arrest you for obstruction of justice and you will accompany us to the nearest police station for questioning.'

'Great. Let's go. My being dressed like this will give the boys at the cop shop a treat.'

Delyse said, 'We will give you time to get dressed.'

The woman looked at Delyse and said, 'As you are black with a Caribbean accent I'm guessing we are fellow immigrants to this ridiculous country so, as a fellow outsider, I will let you in to answer your questions. Please make it quick. I have had a busy night.'

The woman led them down the hallway and into a well-furnished and cosy living room. She switched off the television and invited them to sit down on a sofa while she took an armchair. She picked up a glass of gin and tonic from a side table and asked, 'Would you like a drink?'

'No thank you,' Delyse said, more primly than intended. 'We are on duty.'

The woman looked at her and said, 'How much do you earn for doing your duty? You are very attractive. With my contacts and guidance you could increase your salary several times.'

Before Delyse could answer, Rossi asked, 'What is your name?'

'Magda Lepinski.'

'Where are you from, Magda?'

'I am from Czechoslovakia but my father was Polish. We moved to England after the Russians crushed the Prague Spring in 1968. I was twenty years of age. It is all legal. I have the documents to prove it.'

'We are not concerned about your immigration status,' Rossi said. 'What do you do for a living?'

'I am a prostitute,' Magda said, without a hint of embarrassment or shame. She smiled at Rossi. 'My rates are reasonable, especially for a good-looking boy like you.'

Rossi tried not to colour up. 'We are not concerned with your livelihood, albeit in an oblique way. Were you trafficked? Was your move to England arranged by criminals?'

'No,' Magda protested hotly. 'I moved here with my family. I was not trafficked. I offer special services to a special list of clients. I do not solicit, keep a brothel or walk the streets. I am a high-class whore. I was lucky enough to be born beautiful with a great body and a loathing of hard work. What is your fantasy, Sergeant Rossi? Bondage? Role play? Oral?'

Delyse said, 'We are not interested in your services. We are interested in your last visitor.'

'What about him?'

'Do you know who he is?'

'Yes, he is Baby Bad Boy.'

Delyse looked at Rossi, then Magda. 'What do you mean, Baby Bad Boy?'

'That is how he likes to be known when I "entertain" him. He is a bad little boy who has soiled his nappy. I take away his dummy and punish him. He has his tantrum and I breast feed him to placate him before the happy ending.'

Rossi asked, 'Do you mean he actually soils his . . .?'

'No, you idiot,' Magda laughed. 'It is role play, fantasy, illusion.'

Rossi cleared his throat. 'Do you know his real identity?'

Magda shrugged. 'Colonel Latimer he calls himself. Whether that is his real name or not I don't care, as long as he pays.'

'That is his real name,' Delyse confirmed. 'Are you aware of his position in society?'

'Do you mean his career?'

'In a way. Colonel Latimer is Deputy Lord Lieutenant of Bedfordshire.'

Magda took a sip of gin. 'Sounds grand but I have no idea what that means.'

'It means he is the monarch's deputy representative for official and ceremonial duties in the county of Bedfordshire.'

Magda shrugged. 'So what? Your ridiculous snobby English customs are of no interest to me.'

Rossi asked, 'When you are not entertaining Colonel Latimer as his baby personae, do you talk him as a normal human being?'

'Yes, of course. I quite like the man. He is well-mannered, polite, well-dressed, clean. I wish I could say that about all my clients.'

'Such as Charlie Falconer?' Delyse ventured.

Magda did not betray any reaction to the name. 'I don't know who that is, unless one of my clients is also using a false name.'

'Falconer is a London gangster. Do you think any of your clients could be a criminal?'

'I don't think so. My clients are ordinary, albeit wealthy men, who wish to indulge their fantasies in a discreet and secure environment.'

'We shall need a list of all your clients,' Delyse said.

'I don't have one.'

'Then we shall obtain a warrant to seize your records,'

'That is not possible unless you seize me. My records are in my head. Nothing is written down.'

'Then you must write them down on paper for us,' Rossi said.

'As you English say, not on your nelly. I will not divulge details about my clients, even if you torture me. That is an assurance I promise my clients and that is why I have flourished, and become moderately wealthy, in my chosen profession.'

Rossi asked, 'What can you tell us about Colonel Latimer as a person?'

'In what way do you mean?'

'Are you aware he is married for instance? Does his wife know about his relationship with you?'

Magda shrugged. 'I don't know. I shouldn't think so. He once told me he was happily married. It was only his sexual kink that could not be satisfied in that relationship.'

'Anything you can tell us about his life or opinions?' Delyse asked. 'Any information might help us?'

'Why should I help you get Latimer arrested? I would be cutting off an income stream.' Magda smiled wryly.

'There is no question of Colonel Latimer being arrested, or even getting into trouble,' Rossi said.

'Yes,' Delyse said. 'We are trying to help Colonel Latimer. We suspect he is being used and manipulated by person or persons unknown.'

'Like that Falconer man you mentioned?'

'Yes. Falconer is a dangerous man.'

Magda's attitude softened. 'The only thing I can tell you is about politics. Latimer is genuinely interested in my background in fleeing from Communist oppression. He would rant about the state of this country. He hates Margaret Thatcher.'

'That's surprising,' Delyse said. 'I would have thought Latimer was a natural Tory, a supporter of Thatcher.'

'It was the Falklands War that turned him against Thatcher. All those young men, British and Argentine, killed. Latimer, being an ex-army man, thought it all could have been avoided if the government had been tougher and shrewder in the first place.'

'I agree with that,' Rossi said.

'Did you serve in the war?'

'No, but my brother did. He never came home.'

'Then I am truly sorry,' Magda said. 'When the IRA bombed the Grand Hotel last year and nearly killed Thatcher, Latimer was sorry they failed. It was a wicked thing to say and I told him so. He also supported the miners during their strike. Latimer said that he comes from a working class background despite his rank and appearance. He deeply admires what that man Kinnock is doing to the Labour Party by ejecting the Communist element to make them electable.'

'Well,' Rossi said. 'The dear Colonel is full of surprises.'

Magda asked, 'Are you going to tell him that you interrogated me tonight?'

'Not unless it becomes absolutely necessary,' Delyse said. 'It is true that we want to help Latimer. Your arrangement with him is your business and nothing to do with the police.'

Magda nodded. 'That is good.'

'We want you to carry on seeing Colonel Latimer. If you hear him say anything you think might be leading him into trouble then let us know.'

'Especially if he mentions that man Falconer,' Magda said.

'Yes, but do not mention that name to Latimer first or else he will know something is wrong.'

Rossi and Delyse left Magda's bungalow. As they were walking to the car Rossi said, 'Do you believe she knows nothing about Falconer?'

'Yes,' Delyse replied. 'I don't think she was lying. We've certainly unearthed a few skeletons in the Latimer closet tonight.'

22

Rossi and Delyse waited until the car park attendant went back into his kiosk and, crouching low, they slipped past and into the low-ceilinged underground car park. They examined the parked vehicles as they looked for somewhere to conceal themselves.

'There is Turnbull's car,' Delyse whispered. 'Over there, the green Rover.'

'Okay,' Rossi said. 'Let's find somewhere to hide until he appears. He shouldn't be long.'

They found a space in the shadows, well hidden from the street entrance, behind a square concrete pillar. They stood close together.

'This is ridiculous,' Delyse said, uncomfortably brushing against Rossi. 'I hope you've cleaned your teeth today. And used mouthwash.'

'My dental hygiene is immaculate, as is my general hygiene. I'm not keen on your perfume.'

'It's Desiree by Coco Chanel.'

'More like cocoa by English Channel.'

'Very witty. Never mind my perfume. We were ordered not to investigate this case. Why should Turnbull take any notice?'

Rossi shrugged. 'Where else can we go?'

'I feel silly. We should simply go to his office.'

'If we did that in public, Turnbull would be duty bound to report us to our superiors and if he did that we could lose our careers. Despite his personal peccadilloes, Turnbull seems to me a conscientious and committed officer.'

As he spoke, Rossi felt the barrel of a pistol against the back of his head. A voice said, 'It's nice to hear you have a decent opinion of me, sergeant, but may I ask what you two country bumpkins are doing lurking near my car.'

Rossi said, 'Please point that gun away from my head, then we'll tell you.'

'It's not a gun. It's my trusty Parker fountain pen. You can turn around now.'

'How did you see us?' Delyse asked. 'We are well hidden.'

'This car park is often used by Special Branch as well as the general public. There are surveillance cameras. We don't like our officers blithely walking into potential danger spots without some warning. What are you two doing here?' Delyse said, 'We have a tape we want you to listen to.' 'Oh, good,' Turnbull said. 'I like the Beatles. Or that Swedish group with the fancy clothes.'

'This isn't music. It's a conversation. It will only take five minutes. Let's get in your car and I'll play it.'

Turnbull sighed. 'Curiosity overcomes my better judgement. Come on.'

Delyse and Turnbull took the front seats while Rossi leaned in from the back. Delyse took out a portable tape player. She fast forwarded to the conversation. As soon as Turnbull heard the voice he cried, 'That's Charlie Falconer!'

'So it is,' Delyse said. 'Keep listening.'

Delyse switched off the tape. Turnbull leaned back and pursed his lips. 'Who's is the other voice?' he asked.

'That,' Rossi said, 'is the Deputy Lord Lieutenant of my fair county of Bedfordshire, Colonel Latimer.'

'You mean the one who organised the garden party with Falconer and the dead Russian?'

Rossi nodded. 'And including my own Chief Superintendent.'

'Where did you get this recording?' Turnbull demanded. 'How did you get it?'

'I used my initiative,' Delyse answered. 'How or where need not concern you. I swear it is genuine. It proves there is a link between Latimer and Falconer, and not just social chit chat, they are planning something.'

Rossi said, 'From the mention of sex, we suspect they may be trafficking girls into the country.'

'That's a bit of a stretch,' Turnbull said. 'Perhaps it's just local sex trade.'

'The dead Russian may have been involved,' Delyse said. 'And the oh-so-upright Colonel Latimer is regularly visiting a high class whore from eastern Europe.' She related their visit to Magda Lepinski.

'Wait a minute,' Turnbull said. 'Your superiors ordered you off this case. Why are you still investigating and where did you obtain this tape.'

Rossi said, 'We are still investigating because we have a duty as police officers. We came to you to ask if you have any evidence that Charlie Falconer is involved in sex trafficking?'

'Falconer has his sticky greedy fingers in many pies, and no doubt prostitution is one of them, but I'm not aware of any evidence about trafficking from abroad.'

'What about this Railway Tavern they mentioned? Do you know anything about that?'

'No.'

There was silence for several moments. Then Delyse asked, 'What are you going to do? Grass on us to our bosses?'

'Certainly not. I don't know how you obtained this tape and you're obviously not going to tell me. I understand that.'

Rossi said, 'What about Special Branch taking over the case?'

'No. I hate to admit it but Falconer has informants within Special Branch. I'm impressed with what you've found here. I want you to keep investigating. We can't get near Falconer but now you've proved the link with Colonel Latimer, I want you to lean on him, find out what he's up to, but *do not* tell him that you know about Falconer. Investigating the death of the Russian is still sufficient cover. This business of him visiting his whore will give you leverage. He won't want his wife, the saintly Lord Lieutenant, knowing about that. Put the heat on Latimer, see if he slips up.'

'But we've been warned off,' Rossi pointed out.

'If you get trouble from your superiors I'll back you up,' Turnbull promised. 'Now, will you kindly piss off out of my car so I can go home for dinner?'

23

Colonel Hugh Latimer stood up from his desk as the maid ushered Delyse and Rossi into his office. He said, 'Thank you, Olga. Would you please bring a tray of coffee for my guests?'

Delyse said, 'Don't bring us anything, Olga. We won't be taking up much of the Colonel's valuable time.'

Olga nodded and closed the office door as she went out. Latimer gestured to the office chairs in front of his desk. 'Please sit down, sergeants. How can I help you today?'

Rossi said, 'We are still investigating the death of Radomir Simonek, the guest at your garden party on May 18th.'

Latimer nodded. 'I've given it a lot of thought and I cannot add anything to what I've already told you.'

Delyse said, 'We need to ask you a delicate and personal question and we'd appreciate an honest answer. We can help protect you if need be.'

'That's a puzzling statement,' Latimer said. 'Ask away.'

Rossi said, 'Are you being blackmailed or otherwise pressurised to withhold information from us?'

Latimer seemed genuinely puzzled. 'What a strange question! Why, or especially how, would anyone try to blackmail me?'

'Because of your relationship with Magda Lepinski. We understand that you would not want your wife to know about this relationship and we have no intention of telling her if you admit you are being blackmailed because of it.'

Latimer did not reply. Then he leaned forward and pressed an intercom. He said, 'Darling, sorry to disturb you. I have sergeants Rossi and Joseph in my office. They are still investigating the death of Radomir Simonek. Could you join us for a few minutes?'

There was awkward silence until Mrs Latimer entered the office. Rossi stood up. She said, 'No need to get up, sergeant. What can I do for you?'

Before Rossi could reply, the Colonel said, 'They are asking about my arrangement with Magda Lepinski. Would you mind telling them all about it?'

Mrs Latimer's attitude turned frosty as she scowled at Delyse and Rossi. She said, 'My husband visits Ms Lepinski regularly with my full knowledge and permission. She fulfils certain needs my husband requires, which I cannot fulfil, with my blessing. Our marriage is very happy.'

'Thank you for your honesty,' Delyse said.

Mrs Latimer said, 'You may not believe us but we respect the law, as we are duty bound to do by our official positions, and we respect the job you have to do but we had nothing to do with the death of this Radomir Simonek and I will be contacting your superiors to stop this intrusive and unwarranted questioning.'

24

Rossi left Chief Superintendent Pritchard's office and returned to his desk in the squad room. He was thankful the room was deserted except for DC Penhall half asleep over in the opposite corner. He rang Delyse. 'Can you talk?'

'Yes,' Delyse said, 'although Mallick nearly ripped out my tongue when I tried to explain. If we go near the Latimers again I'm off the force.'

'I sympathise,' Rossi said. 'I've just had the biggest bollocking of my life. I was told the same. The Latimers are out of bounds.'

'How can we explain to our guvnors without mentioning Charlie Falconer?'

'We can't. Turnbull was adamant about that.'

'Do we give up?'

'We can't do that either. We owe it to Ivan Doe to find his killer, we owe it to ourselves as committed police officers, and we owe it to the general public to nail Charlie Falconer. At least we have Turnbull secretly backing us.'

Delyse said, 'Turnbull has identified the Railway Tavern as an abandoned pub in Bermondsey. Right in the heart of Falconer territory.'

'Is he putting it under surveillance?'

'No. He said it's deserted, windows boarded up. He claims he hasn't got the resources to watch the place without further definite information.'

'Then let's find that information for him.'

Delyse said sceptically, 'You mean go and examine the place ourselves?'

'Exactly.'

'What if it's being occupied by gangsters or sex traffickers?'

'It's a risk but we know there is something really bad going on, even if our superiors can't see it or accept it. You risked your life in that tacky night club to find us this information. Let's act on it.'

'Very well. Let's do it.'

'That's my girl,' Rossi said.

'That's never going to happen,' Delyse replied.

25

Delyse Joseph said, 'We've been sitting on this park bench for nearly two hours.'

'Just like Darby and Joan,' Rossi said.

'Who are Darby and Joan?'

'An old couple who are the epitome of contented wedded bliss.'

'That will never be us. And don't call me old.' Delyse scrunched up her plastic coffee cup and tossed it into the adjacent waste bin. 'Vile coffee, my jeans probably stained with bird shit from this bench and, worst of all, a lesson in ancient British folklore from you. We've been watching the pub for long enough. Isn't it time we made a move?'

'A few more minutes. Let the light fade a bit more. See if any lights in the pub are switched on.'

'I don't know if you've noticed, Einstein, but the windows are boarded up.'

'We would still see chinks of light.'

'Unlike the recesses of your brain.'

The Railway Tavern was an old Victorian pub, a square building of three stories built around a courtyard which was protected from the outside by a head-height brick wall. The building stood on the corner of a quiet street but was detached from other, later, constructions. The fascia displaying the name Railway Tavern in gold letters on a green background had once been illuminated by a row of brass lamps, now sadly unlit. It was built of red bricks with window and door frames painted white, now peeling, with Dutch-style gables on the top story, the only touch of genteel decoration.

Rossi said, 'There's no sign of life in there. Surely it's now safe to go in and have a look.'

Delyse was suddenly dubious. 'What if a person or persons unknown are squatting in there and we go waltzing in?'

'Then we tell them we are doing the same, looking for a place to squat. In a last resort we flash our warrant cards.'

'Umm. If they are really bad perps, as we suspect, that might get us killed.'

Rossi shrugged. 'Perhaps, but we have to go in. It's our only way forward in the case.'

'Okay,' Delyse said. 'How do we get in?'

'Through those gates in the wall. That's obviously where the drays used to deliver the beer barrels.'

'How do we get over the wall?'

'You give me a leg up, I'll nip over and unlock the gates.'

'What if those gates are securely locked? Why don't we try the front door? If anyway sees us we'll pretend we didn't notice the pub is closed.'

Rossi sighed in exasperation. 'Do you really think that if the bad guys are using the pub for nefarious purposes they would leave the front entrance open for all and sundry to walk in?'

'If they've finished with the place and it's going to be demolished anyway, why not?'

'You're a bloody optimist. Okay, the street is quiet now. Let's go try the door.'

As they stood up Delyse grabbed Rossi's arm and beamed a smile at him.

'What are you doing?' Rossi asked in astonishment.

'Pretending we're a loving couple, wrapped up in each other's company, trying to get a drink and not noticing the pub is derelict.'

'You should be an actress. Or a script writer.'

Dodging the London traffic they crossed the main road and walked nonchalantly up to the front door of the Railway

Tavern. Delyse pushed the door and it opened. She said, 'Quick, get inside.'

They stepped into the dark saloon bar, quietly closed the front door behind them and, for several moments, stopped to listen for sounds of occupancy.

'Told you the door would open,' Delyse said.

'Smart arse,' Rossi retorted, and took out his torch from his jacket pocket. Delyse took out her torch from her anorak jacket pocket. They switched on the torches and illuminated the L-shaped bar area. The cheap wooden tables and chairs were still in place, standing on a grubby green carpet. A juke box and a one-armed bandit stood unlit and gathering dust. All bottles had been removed from behind the bar. They split up to check the ladies and gents lavatories.

'Pretty clean,' Delyse reported. 'It's possible that someone has been staying here recently. Check the cellar. There's a flap in the floor behind the bar here.'

'Why don't you check the cellar? You're wearing jeans and an anorak. I'm wearing a good suit.'

'And very elegant you look. Now, try being a real man and get down that cellar.'

Rossi, grumbling under his breath, gingerly descended a short ladder. 'Hope there's no rats down here, of any kind.' After a few seconds he called up. 'Nothing down here. Everything useful or valuable has been removed.'

'Okay, I've looked in the kitchen area. That's all stripped out. Come back up and let's try the next floor. There's a door marked "private" here.'

Delyse opened the door to find a stairway to the first floor. They went up to a landing with a door marked "Games Room" on the left and another stairway leading up to the top floor.

Rossi opened the games room door. 'Jackpot,' he breathed as they went in. The whole floor was a shabby open plan room with pool and shove ha'penny tables, a dartboard and a large television screen on the wall for showing sports events. Dozens of light metal chairs were stacked around the walls. On the floor were mattresses and sleeping bags. There were six tatty armchairs. Takeaway wrappings, cartons and empty bottles were strewn everywhere.

'Clearly people have been living here,' Delyse said, 'but does it give us any clues. What about that big metal cabinet over there?'

Stepping over the detritus Rossi went over and inspected the cabinet. There were louvred slots at the top of the doors. Rossi shone his torch through them to inspect the interior, then opened the doors. 'Nothing,' he pronounced. 'Completely empty.'

Delyse was kneeling down. 'Let's sort through this disgusting mess. We may find something of value.'

Rossi said, 'I'll go up to the top floor. It's usually the landlord's private quarters.' He returned minutes later. 'The whole place is stripped of any furniture or bedding, but the shower and basin and lavatory facilities have definitely been used recently. So has the small kitchen up there. Now we have to establish who they were?'

'Okay. Hold your nose and help me sort through this bedding.'

Suddenly there was noise from downstairs. A door banged shut, voices shouting and laughing. Rossi and Delyse looked at each other as they tried to hear what was going on. The voices became louder. The stairs creaked.

'Sounds like several men. They're coming up the stairs,' Delyse whispered. 'What do we do?'

'We'll get in the metal locker. Perhaps they won't stay long, whoever they are.'

'You're joking. That locker is hardly big enough for one and we're bound to make a noise.'

'Any better ideas?'

'No,' Delyse conceded. 'Let's get in.'

They squeezed into the locker, having to stand face-to-face. Rossi managed to silently close the doors as someone switched on the lights. Light flooded through the louvred vents in the locker. Rossi peered out. Six men aged twenties to forties, tough looking, casually dressed, entered the games room. They were carrying bottles and cans, some were smoking cigarettes, all in high spirits, laughing and ribbing each other. One of them opened the doors of the dartboard cabinet. Another man put an LP record on a cheap Dansette record player. Some sort of ethnic folk music.

'Good,' whispered Rossi, directly in Delyse's face. 'That'll help cover our noise.'

'They sound Russian,' Delyse whispered back. 'Move your elbow, its digging in me.'

'I can't,' Rossi hissed. 'Hope they don't smell your perfume.'

'Hope they don't smell your breath.'

Rossi twisted his neck and again peered out of the louvred slots. 'Let's observe as much as we can. We might recognise them afterwards.'

'If we survive.'

A darts game had started. Someone had chalked the names of two teams on the scoreboard. The standard of play was appalling and no-one seemed to know the rules, or how to count up, or even care.

Rossi whispered, 'Not all Russian. Two sound Irish or Cockney.'

Delyse nodded. 'Can't make out what they're saying.'

The game and the noise and the excessive drinking went on for over an hour. Then a telephone rang. The record player was switched off and one of the men answered the phone. He listened and said several words, which sounded like Russian, then turned to his companions and said another few words in a serious tone. The men reluctantly abandoned their drinks and filed out of the games room.

Delyse and Rossi waited, stock still, until they were certain the men were out of earshot. They stepped out of the locker and took deep breaths of the fuggy air.

'What do we do now?' Rossi asked.

'Keep looking for evidence,' Delyse said.

Rossi went to the dartboard and examined the scoreboard. 'Look at these team names. Looks like "cokon" and "33k". Does that mean anything to you?'

'Not a thing,' Delyse said. 'They were all so drunk they didn't know what they were writing. Let's keep looking through the bedding. I'll look down the stairs to make sure they have all gone.' She carefully opened the door and let out an involuntary cry of horror.

'What is it?' Rossi said, rushing to her side. He looked down at the wall of fire flicking and swirling its way up the stairs. He shut the door tightly and said, 'We are in big trouble. They've finished using the pub as a base so they're torching the evidence.'

Delyse went to the window and looked down into the courtyard. 'There's the roof of the kitchen extension below and off to the left. We would have to swing across but we may be able to get out this way.' She attempted to lift the sash window. 'Damn, this window is stuck shut.' She looked back to see Rossi lifting the dartboard cabinet off its brackets. 'What are you doing?'

Rossi walked to the window and, using the cabinet for protection, charged with his shoulder. The glazing bars broke, shattered glass fell everywhere. He threw the cabinet down to the courtyard below. 'Saving the evidence,' he explained. He grabbed the sash window and, loosened by the shock of Rossi's charge, it flew up easily.

Acrid smoke was now billowing in under the door, fanned by the air flow from the open window. The paint on the door was peeling from the heat on the other side.

'I'll go out first,' Rossi said, climbing out of the window.

'Such a gentleman! What happened to women and children first?'

'If I can make it on to that roof I can help you across, save you from falling.'

'What if you don't make it?'

'Ever the bloody optimist. I'll make it. I want to know what those pesky Russians are up to.'

The games room door caught fire.

'Go,' Delyse said, almost pushing Rossi out of the window.

Rossi ducked out and balanced precariously on the window ledge. There was a cast iron drainpipe within reach. Rossi reached out and grabbed the bracket. He swung himself out and grabbed the bracket with his other hand. Bracing his legs on the wall he jumped towards the slanting slate roof of the outhouse. He landed with a painful thump but managed to hold on to stop himself rolling off. He looked back to see Delyse climbing out of the window. The flames were chasing behind her.

Rossi braced himself as Delyse swung herself on to the drain pipe. She caught her breath for a second and then threw herself towards the outhouse roof. She fell short with one leg dangling but Rossi grabbed the hood of her anorak and pulled her to safety. They held each other, recovering strength and breath.

'What now, Tarzan,' Delyse asked.

'It's still a way down from here but there are some old beer crates over there. I'll scramble down the kitchen drainpipe and build you a platform to get down.'

'Why do I need you to build me a platform? I can shin down the drainpipe as well as you can.'

'Women's lib gone mad,' Rossi said, and climbed down to the ground. He looked up to see flames shooting out of the games room window. 'Come on,' he shouted, 'let's get away from here in case anything explodes.'

Rossi picked up the darts cabinet while Delyse shinned down the drainpipe. The evening air was filling with the sound of fire service and police sirens. The courtyard gate was bolted but not padlocked. Rossi forced open the bolt and they stepped out on to the street. A small crowd had already gathered to watch the fire. A few people looked at Delyse and Rossi curiously but no-one said anything or attempted to stop them.

'Typically British,' Delyse said as they walked off. 'Come on, let's get away. Best if nobody connects us with the fire. It would be difficult to explain what we are doing to the police. You know how suspicious and obnoxious those coppers can be.'

26

Commander Turnbull stood up from his desk. He sighed heavily and went to the window to observe the busy London thoroughfare below Scotland Yard while he contemplated the situation. Eventually he turned to look at Delyse and Rossi and said, 'I can't decide if you are genuinely devoted police officers with commendable initiative or bullshitting liars who are in the pay of criminals in order to put me off the scent. You expect me to believe that you concealed yourselves, undiscovered, in a cupboard while Russian gangsters played darts outside?'

Delyse said, 'We expect you to believe it because it's the truth.'

Rossi added, 'The pub has burned to the ground. Isn't that true?'

'You could have torched the place yourselves.'

Delyse said, 'We are being patient with you, Commander, because of your low regard for we straw-munching country coppers, but we have evidence and you must listen to us.'

Turnbull bristled. 'You're telling a Special Branch commander that he must listen to you. You're over-reaching, young lady.'

'Don't call me "young lady". I am a detective sergeant in Hertfordshire constabulary. I demand my respect as well as you do.'

Turnbull grunted and pointed to the bubble-wrapped parcel leaning against the side of his desk. 'Is that your evidence, in there?'

'Yes,' Rossi said. He picked up the parcel and carefully unwrapped the darts scoreboard. He laid it on Turnbull's desk. 'This is from the dartboard cabinet in the Railway Tavern. You may be able to take fingerprints.'

'Did you also pick up the darts or the chalk? More likely to have prints on them.'

'There wasn't time,' Rossi said. 'This was the best we could do before burning to death.'

Turnbull leaned over and perused the scoreboard. 'Nothing here to worry Eric Bristow. Not very good darts players.'

'They were very drunk,' Delyse said.

'Darts players usually are. These scores are written in standard Arabic numbers. Nothing to deduce from them.'

'It's the team names we were interested in,' Rossi said. 'They look as if they could be Russian but we're not sure.'

'Umm,' Turnbull said. He picked up the telephone and dialled a number. 'Ask Mary to come to my office right away please.'

Delyse asked, 'Who is Mary?'

'Mary is my best Russian language expert. Lived undercover in Moscow for many years and passed as Russian without any problems.'

Five minutes later Mary entered the office. He was a tall, slim elegantly dressed gentleman in his fifties. His hair was turning grey but was still thick and well-styled. His shirt cuffs were turned back over the sleeves of his powder blue suit. The smell of his aftershave and other unguents filled Turnbull's office.

Turnbull said, 'This is Special Agent Martin Goodhew, known affectionately as Mary. Stole secrets from under the noses of the Bolsheviks for years without them ever suspecting.'

'They could not believe a scented old poof would outwit them,' Mary smiled.

Turnbull said, 'Mary, please take a look at this scoreboard and see if they mean anything in regard to Russia.'

Mary put his arms behind his back and leaned over to study the board. Suddenly he straightened up. 'Where did this come from?'

Turnbull replied, 'For the moment, Mary, you do not need to know. What can you tell us?'

'Of course, Commander. My apologies.' He pointed to the right hand row of scores. 'This row of figures is headed by the Russian word meaning "falcon".'

'The word that looks like "cokon" you mean,' Rossi asked, hardly daring to breathe.

'Yes,' Mary replied. 'This other heading is very interesting. It looks like "33k" in English but in Russian Cyrillic it means "zek".'

Turnbull said, 'Oh, my God,' and turned back to look out the window.

Delyse asked, 'What does zek mean?'

Mary said, 'Zek, spelt z-e-k in English, refers to a class of prisoner in the Soviet Union.'

'You mean criminals?' Rossi asked.

'Perhaps, or more usually political prisoners. The prison camps, the Gulags, were trawled by the KGB to find men who spoke English and who could be trained to come to the UK, legally or illegally, and foment trouble in any way they could, especially with the help of unwitting British Communist fellow travellers.'

Delyse said, 'Why should they bother with their insidious tasks once they arrive in Britain? They could ask for asylum and be free.'

'Because the Soviet authorities threaten that their loved ones, family, children, etcetera, will be killed or imprisoned if they do not execute their orders.'

Rossi said, 'But what if. . .'

Turnbull said, 'That's enough for now. Thank you, Mary. You can go now and do not mention what you have seen to anyone.'

'Of course, Commander,' Mary said, and quietly left the office.

Turnbull returned to his desk and sat down. 'Very well, you two are right. The reference to Falcon is clearly a link with Charlie Falconer and if zeks are involved there must be something highly dangerous going on.'

Delyse said, 'So when we thought these men were saying "sex" it must have been "zeks".'

Turnbull nodded. 'Leave the scoreboard with me. I'll get it forensically analysed for fingerprints.'

'What can we do now?' Delyse asked.

'I want you to go back and interrogate this Deputy Lord Lieutenant chap, Latimer. He's obviously involved in this somehow. Rather than Special Branch bursting in on him, he won't be suspecting you know about his involvement with Falconer and zeks. I want you to make him sweat. With any luck he'll crack and admit what is going on. I'll get a warrant to tap his telephone.'

Delyse and Rossi made to get up but Turnbull said, 'Stay there for the moment.' He unlocked a desk drawer and took out a box file. He slid it across the desk and said, 'These are all the surveillance photographs, and photographs taken by local press snappers, from the May 18th garden party.'

'I thought there was only one photograph,' Rossi said.

'You didn't need to know about these until now. Look through them carefully and see if you can identify anyone who might have been at that pub darts game, or anything else that might be useful and indicative. Hand me that bubble wrap.' Turnbull carefully rewrapped the scoreboard. 'I'll take this to forensics now. Study those photographs here for as long as you like. Don't try to search my office because everything vital is under lock and key.'

131

Turnbull left.

'Such a pleasant trusting man,' Rossi said.

'At least he's willing to listen to us now.' Delyse picked up the box file and withdrew the stack of photographs of the party. 'You have half and I'll have half and then we'll swap over.'

'Yes, mam,' Rossi said. He switched on Turnbull's desk lamp.

'Are your eyes bad?' Delyse asked.

'Yes, they've been dazzled by your beauty.'

'Of course. Get studying.'

After half an hour of searching, Delyse had laid two photos aside and Rossi had also laid two aside. Rossi said, 'I can't identify anyone from the pub but there is something odd in these two shots.'

Delyse picked up her two photos and said, 'I know what you are going to say.'

They examined all four together. Delyse said, 'Definitely highly suspicious.'

27

Colonel Hugo Latimer, Deputy Lord Lieutenant of Bedfordshire, did a fine job of hiding his irritation as he showed Delyse and Rossi into his office at The Mallows. He indicated for his visitors to sit down and said, 'You two are persistent, I'll give you that. Have you identified the dead Russian yet?'

'No,' Delyse said. 'We want you to tell us who he really is.'

Latimer pretended bafflement. 'Me? How should I know?'

Rossi said, 'Because you are involved in a scheme to import Russian prisoner thugs, known as zeks, into Britain.'

Latimer did another fine job of hiding his surprise but the sudden tension in his eyes and his manner told Delyse and Rossi the bare statement had packed a massive clout. Latimer said, lamely, 'I'm afraid I don't know what you are talking about.'

Delyse said, 'We have proof you are colluding with a gangster named Charlie Falconer to form a group of zeks for some criminal purpose. The jig is up, Colonel Latimer. Now you must tell us all you know about this scheme.'

The name Falconer caused Latimer's eyes to widen even further. 'I have no idea what you mean?'

'Tell you what,' Delyse said. 'My colleague and I are rather thirsty. How about ordering us a pot of tea?'

Now Latimer was completely off balance. He picked up the phone and said, 'Pot of tea for two in my office please.' Before he could put the phone down, Rossi said, 'A biscuit or two wouldn't go amiss.'

Latimer ordered biscuits and replaced the receiver. 'Either you two are taking drugs or you seriously wish to ruin whatever careers you have left. Sergeant Rossi, I know your superior officer very well. I'll be interested to hear what Chief Superintendent Pritchard has to say about your insane accusations.'

Rossi said, 'I'm aware, of course, that Pritchard attended your garden party in May. He's a friend as well as my superior but your criminal plot has now gone way above his pay grade and up to a Commander in Special Branch. It will go a lot easier to tell us what you are planning before the heavies get involved. A full confession now may get you a reduced sentence. With savage Russian trained convicts involved I'm sure you are not planning to raid the church tombola takings.'

Latimer sat back and pretended to think. Then he said, 'I have no idea what you are talking about.'

A light knock on the door and Olga the maid entered carrying a tray of tea and biscuits. She set down the tray on the desk and made to leave.

Delyse said, 'Olga, please join us for a cup of tea. Pull up a chair and make yourself comfortable.'

Olga, flustered, looked at Latimer. He shrugged and said, 'Do as she asks.'

Olga pulled up a chair and perched timidly on the edge.

Rossi stood up and said, 'I'll be mother. Anyone take sugar? Help yourself.' He poured three cups and selected a Rich Tea biscuit.

Delyse took a cup and said, 'Well, this is nice. Olga, how is your sister?'

Olga's eyes widened. 'I have not got a sister.'

'Oh, come now,' Delyse continued. 'It's natural to be a little ashamed of what she does for a living but we liked her. An honest and up front lady.'

'I don't. . .'

'Yes,' Rossi interrupted. 'You and Magda have done well since fleeing to the UK. Magda has kept her real surname, Lepinski, but you changed yours. Surveillance photographs of your little "soiree" show from the body language that you and the Deputy Lord Lieutenant here have a much more intimate and personal relationship than maid and master. You put him in contact with your sister and your knowledge of Slavic languages must be very useful in the recruitment of zeks from Russia and eastern Europe.'

At the mention of the word zeks, Olga turned to Latimer in panic.

'Say nothing, Olga,' Latimer barked. 'These officers are throwing false accusations at us, for what reason I don't know.'

Delyse leaned forward towards Olga. 'Tell us everything you know and we can protect you from the zeks and from Charlie Falconer.'

Olga said to Latimer, 'We must tell them.'

'No!' Latimer shouted. 'They have no proof of these insane accusations.'

'Are you sure of that?' Rossi said.

'If you had we would already be behind bars. Olga, the law requires proof before conviction of a crime, not wild threats from renegade rural coppers.'

Olga put her head down and whispered, 'I can tell you nothing.'

There was silence for a few moments. Delyse said, 'Very well, if you two insist on remaining silent we have to report to Special Branch that you refused to co-operate. You will at least be charged with obstruction of justice.'

Latimer said, 'Do what you have to do, sergeant.' He said the word "sergeant" with a sneer.

Rossi stood up. 'Excellent biscuits,' he said.

28

Chief Superintendent Pritchard realised he had made the biggest mistake of his life. He had destroyed his career, his reputation, any possibility of future employment, and possibly his marriage and the respect of his children. He looked up at the bare ceiling and beige walls of the interview room, anything to avoid the gaze of Commander Turnbull and Sergeants Rossi and Joseph. Pritchard was trapped. There was no excuse that would make any sense, so he decided to tell the truth. At least that would salvage some pride and decency, if only in his own mind.

Rossi asked, 'How did it happen that you turned up, in full uniform, at the Road Star Lodge, early in the morning, to the scene of what was ostensibly a common unexplained sudden death?'

Pritchard took a deep breath. 'I was paid to go there.'

'You mean bribed?' Delyse asked.

'If you like. Paid, bribed, it doesn't matter.'

'Who bribed you?' Turnbull asked.

'The money came through Latimer, the Deputy Lord Lieutenant, but I think the source of the money was someone else.'

'Charlie Falconer?' Turnbull said.

'I don't know,' Pritchard answered hotly. 'I didn't know Falconer was at that garden party. I didn't know who he was. I don't know about these London bigshots. I'm a provincial copper.'

'Correction,' Turnbull said. 'You *were* a provincial copper. You're no sort of copper from now on, so you might as well help us and tell the truth. Your co-operation will be considered in any jail sentence you receive.'

'I will tell you the truth,' Pritchard said, head bowed.

Rossi asked: 'So you were paid to attend the scene of the Russian's death, but why? What was the point of you turning up?'

'I was to make sure that all the Russians belongings had been taken away and that no clues as to his identity were left behind. I was also to obstruct the investigation as much as I could without making it obvious. That was made much easier when I found out both Sergeant Rossi and Sergeant Joseph had been sent on the same case. I arranged for you two to work together thinking that you would detest each other and want to get the investigation over with as quickly as possible. Sergeant Rossi knows I have a wry and impish sense of humour so he wouldn't be too suspicious of my little prank.'

Delyse and Rossi looked at each other. Then Delyse asked Pritchard, 'How much were you paid for this little errand?'

'Life changing money. I'd been a copper for years and, despite what you think, always honest, and what had I got for it?'

'How much?' Delyse repeated.

'£100,000.'

Turnbull whistled softly. 'That is big bucks. That must have come from Falconer.'

'And it shows just how important the dead Russian must have been,' Delyse observed.

Turnbull said, 'So where are the zeks?'

Pritchard said, 'What are zeks?'

'The Russian gangsters who were hiding out in the Railway Tavern before it was burned down.'

'I have no idea what you are talking about,' Pritchard insisted.

'Come on, you must tell us what is going on. What nefarious scheme is this gang of Gulag sweepings involved in?'

137

Pritchard shook his head. 'You've lost me completely.'

Half an hour later Pritchard was escorted from the interview room and back to the holding cell.

Turnbull said, 'Sergeant Rossi, you know Pritchard better than we do. Was he telling the truth? Does he really know nothing about the zeks ploy, whatever it is?'

'I do believe him because whoever is masterminding this plot had no need to tell Pritchard. Pritchard was a useful tool, a patsy to muddy the waters of the dead Russian investigation.'

Turnbull shrugged. 'Between us we have interviewed everyone who was at that garden party, everyone we could identify that is. I was hoping Latimer might crack when you confronted him but no luck. I can't get near Falconer.'

Delyse said, 'So where do we go from here?'

Turnbull grinned. 'Let's get Mary in here. I think he may have a little light reading for you.'

Turnbull used the interview room wall phone to make a couple of calls. He replaced the receiver and said, 'You might as well stay here. I've ordered coffee and sandwiches for you.'

Minutes later Mary came in carrying a folder and two ring binders filled with photographs. He put them down on the interview table.

Turnbull said, 'Mary has been heading up our surveillance on this job because of his knowledge of Russia and the Russian language. He might look like an effete upper class twit but is knowledge is as deadly as an Uzi machine gun.'

Mary smiled sweetly. 'So kind of you to say so, Commander. In these ring folders are surveillance photographs of known Russian agents operating in Britain. It's unlikely that the zeks we are seeking will be in this lot because we suspect they are newly arrived but it's worth a try. So, sergeants, we want you to have a pleasant afternoon

138

staring at some really nasty characters and see if you recognise anyone from the Railway Tavern fire.'

Rossi sighed. 'Can't think of a better way to spend an afternoon.'

'That's excellent,' Mary said. 'Now, Commander, our phone taps have yielded nothing of value except a very suspicious call, in English, from an unknown source, to Colonel Latimer.' From the folder, Mary took a transcript of the call and handed it to Turnbull.

Turnbull read aloud: '"Project brought forward. Consignment arrives today at six a.m." No response from Latimer. Umm. They, whoever they are, clearly know they are being watched and that we know they are up to something. If the "project" is being brought forward they are aware they have to hurry before we find out what's going on.'

Delyse pulled a ring binder towards her and shoved the other one in front of Rossi. 'Let's get on with the identity parade.'

Mary handed Turnbull the folder and said, 'These are surveillance photos of all the Soviet Union nationals who have entered the UK legally in the last twenty four hours.'

Turnbull took out the reports and riffled through them. He handed them to the sergeants. 'Have a quick look at those before the ring binders. I doubt any legitimate travellers will be involved in the zeks plan but it's worth a look.'

Delyse took the photographs. At the third photograph she handed it, without a word, to Rossi. 'That's one of them,' Rossi confirmed. 'I'd recognise that bulbous nose and dodgy haircut anywhere.'

Turnbull and Mary were staring at them in amazement. 'Are you sure he was at the Railway Tavern?'

'No doubt,' Delyse said. 'Valentin Berisov, 39, from a place called Khimki.'

'That's near Moscow,' Mary said. 'Is there a surveillance report. Did our boys follow him and find out where he is staying?'

Delyse turned the page. 'Yes, he checked into the Ariel Hotel, Heathrow this morning after he arrived at . . . six a.m.'

29

Valentin Berisov lay on the bed and put his hands behind his head. To the two men searching his hotel room he said, in guttural but passable English, 'You have searched my body. You are searching my belongings. If you would tell me what you are searching for, perhaps I can help you?'

Commander Turnbull looked at Berisov disdainfully but did not reply. To Rossi he said, 'Let's go out to the corridor.' To the two armed police officers guarding Berisov he said, 'Watch him like a hawk. Don't let him get up off that bed.'

Outside, Turnbull said, 'Nothing. Not a damned thing. I don't believe it.'

Rossi said, 'I still think we should have let him run and lead us to the others.'

'We couldn't take that chance,' Turnbull said irritably. 'He's our only solid potential lead.'

'Perhaps his arrival is a coincidence. Perhaps he has nothing to do with the zeks or Latimer.'

The lift doors opened. Delyse and Mary stepped out. Delyse said, 'Berisov is involved alright. Look what we found in his hire car.' She held up a clear plastic bag containing a high velocity sniper rifle. Mary help up a large envelope. 'And these are directions to his target.'

'Let me see,' Turnbull said, almost snatching the envelope away from Mary. He examined the several sheets of paper, mostly in Russian script but with a map of a town included. 'This is a map of Blackpool. What is happening in Blackpool?'

Mary replied, 'It's the Tory party conference very soon.'

'Of course,' Turnbull said. 'The Iron Lady. Margaret Thatcher. Could this be another attempt to assassinate her?'

Mary said, 'Yes, I've only quickly scanned the Russian text but that's the import of how it reads.'

'She's made enough enemies,' Rossi observed. 'Russians, Argentinians, Irish, British miners, take your pick. I wouldn't be surprised if the assassins are lining up.'

Turnbull asked, 'Have either of you two had firearms training?'

'No,' Rossi said.

'Yes,' Delyse said.

'Okay. Sergeant Joseph, when we go back in that room, you take one of the police officer's guns. I'll dismiss them. We don't want anyone to know about this assassination attempt other than ourselves.'

As they re-entered the hotel room, Rossi said to Delyse in amazement, 'You know how to handle a gun?'

'Yes.' Delyse smiled. 'That's got you worried. A girl like me never knows when she might meet a racist psycho prejudiced against women, black people and coppers.'

Turnbull dismissed the two policemen and told Berisov to stay on the bed or else he would be shot. Turnbull sat down at the end of the double bed. Delyse and Mary took the armchairs while Rossi perched on the cheap dressing table.

'We found these in your hire car,' Turnbull began. 'Why would you need a sniper rifle and a map of Blackpool if, as you claim, you are here to enjoy the sights of London.'

Berisov did not reply.

'We know about the gang of zeks gathered by Colonel Latimer and Charlie Falconer. This rifle and these pages suggest that the target is the assassination of Prime Minister Thatcher. Is that so?'

It seemed as if Berisov was not going to reply again but then he said, 'Yes, that is so.'

'It was to take place at the Conservative Party conference in Blackpool?'

'That was considered the easiest way but the zeks are under orders to kill Thatcher wherever and whenever. If they do, they can return to Russia with wealth and honours. If not, they will be killed themselves or returned to the Gulags in Siberia where they come from.'

Rossi asked, 'Was this scheme Colonel Latimer's idea?'

'Yes. He hates Thatcher, for some reason, but he did not have the money or the contacts to recruit the zeks.'

'Who did?' Turnbull asked. 'Was it the gangster, Charlie Falconer?'

Berisov nodded. 'Yes. He is being bankrolled by the Soviet government to the tune of several millions of pounds. Falconer knew it would be a risky assignment but he could not turn down that sort of money.'

'Would you testify in court to that fact?' Turnbull asked.

'I will, if I am granted asylum and protection in the UK. I do not want to go back to Khimki. I want to stay here, in London. I want fine food, fine clothes, and fine women, not tractors and soup.'

Turnbull pretended to consider. 'As long as you tell us all you know, we will consider your application for asylum with due seriousness but that decision is way above my pay grade. If you co-operate with us at Special Branch, I promise we will do our best to favour your application.'

Delyse said, 'I have a question. Is the Lord Lieutenant, Mrs Latimer, involved in this plot?'

Berisov laughed. 'No. She thinks that her husband's only vice is with the prostitute, Magda Lepinski, who is also wholly innocent. Magda's sister Olga, however, is a prime mover in the plot. Mrs Latimer was a very useful patsy to cover our tracks. You British worship these minor aristocrats and can never believe they can do anything evil.'

Rossi asked, 'What do you know about the dead man found at the Road Star Lodge with all his clothes and belongings missing. What was that all about?'

143

'He was one of the zeks. We suspected he was going to defect and ask for asylum, just as I am doing. We were ordered to get rid of him and any evidence of who he was.'

'Who was he?' Delyse asked.

'His name was Ivan Morozov.'

Delyse looked at Rossi. 'We were right about the first name.'

Turnbull said, 'Okay, who are these zeks and where can we find them. I want to stop this insane plot before it gets any further.'

Berisov shrugged. 'That has effectively been done. Now you know that Thatcher is the target she will be doubly guarded.'

'That is so,' Turnbull agreed. 'I assume that you have just returned from Moscow with final orders from your superiors who conceived this mad plot, so now give me the names and whereabouts of the zeks.'

'I cannot do that.'

'If you want asylum I suggest you try harder.'

'I do not know their names and certainly not their whereabouts. Contact is made by a series of cut-outs and passed along like links in a chain.'

'Are you telling me there is no way to stop the assassination scheme going ahead?'

'Oh, I can stop it but I have to ring a certain number given to me by Moscow. I do not know who this person is but they can pass on the message to stop the plot.'

'Very well,' Turnbull said, 'let's do it. Hand me the phone please, sergeant.' Rossi gave Turnbull the phone. It was a cheap push button phone in drab two-tone browns. Turnbull placed it on the bedside cabinet. He said, 'I should warn you that Mary here is fluent in Russian and other Cyrillic languages, so if you say anything other than what we expect to hear you will be arrested and thrown into a cell. Co-operate and you will be taken to a comfortable safe house.'

Berisov nodded. 'I understand.' He lifted the receiver and punched in the phone number. He spoke a few sentences and replaced the receiver.

Mary interpreted. He said: "Operation Magnet has been discovered and betrayed. Disperse and make your ways home. Moscow will not punish you for something not your fault".'

'There,' Berisov said. 'It is over.'

Turnbull stood up and called the two police officers back into the room. Delyse handed back the gun. Turnbull ordered the officers to handcuff Berisov and take him down to the car. 'I'll be down in a few minutes.'

Turnbull, smiling hugely, turned to Delyse and Rossi. 'Congratulations, sergeants. You two have done an excellent job and your superiors will be made fully aware of your contribution. You are now free to return to your homes and normal duties with the thanks of Special Branch. Come, Mary, let's get Berisov to the safe house and continue the interrogation.'

Delyse and Rossi were left to stare at the closing door.

30

Clifton Rossi gunned the engine of the Lancia and turned on to the A10 towards Hertford. 'Man,' he said, 'I'm still buzzing. What have we just done, eh? Bought down a Soviet assassination plot. Not bad for a pair of rustic rozzers. This has got to be worth a promotion to Inspector if Turnbull gives us our due credit.'

Delyse did not say anything. Rossi glanced at her. He could feel her tension. He glanced at his watch. Already well after midnight. Perhaps his partner was simply tired. Thinking of which, he said, 'Any chance I can doss down in your front room again, save me driving all the way back to Bedford.'

'Yes,' Delyse said dully. 'Yes, that'll be okay. Dad will be pleased to see you again.'

'And what a story we've got to tell him, how his little girl and her handsome suave partner defeated the mighty Soviet empire and saved the life of our Prime Minister.'

Delyse did not respond.

Rossi slowed the car and said, 'Okay, I'm no expert on mood and body language but I thought you'd be flying on adrenaline after our adventure today. Well, technically yesterday, but it's simpler to talk about. . .'

'Oh, for God's sake shut up,' Delyse snapped.

'I don't understand,' Rossi said hesitantly. 'Aren't you happy?'

'No. I hate to harsh your mellow, sergeant, but something is wrong.'

'What is this? Some sort of female intuition or . . .'

'It was too easy.'

'Err, what was?'

'Everything about this assassination plot was initially shrouded in secrecy, as you would expect, but then Berisov flies back to Britain without any attempt to disguise who he is. He's known to Special Branch and HM Customs and Excise. He must have expected to be spotted, watched and followed, let alone arrested. He made no attempt to leave his hotel before he was nabbed, made no attempt to hire a car in other than his own name. Then he spills the beans to us about the entire plot with hardly any pressure being exerted. It's like he wanted to be caught.'

'You mean causing a diversion from the real purpose of the plot?'

'Exactly. Berisov is a shrewd, cunning and well-trained Soviet operative. He could have avoided our grasp if he really wanted to.'

'No, no,' Rossi said hotly. 'You're reading this situation all wrong. Berisov wants asylum in Britain, that's why he allowed himself to be captured and was telling us everything.'

'Perhaps, but he risks incurring the wrath of the Soviet authorities, his fellow zeks and bastards like Charlie Falconer. He handed over the goodies with hardly a thought. They knew the plot had been blown. We confronted Colonel Latimer and Olga, Turnbull had pulled in your boss Pritchard and loads of others who were at the garden party. This would be a good way of diverting us from the real purpose of the plot.'

Rossi snorted. 'You've been a copper for years, same as me. Sometimes we get lucky, sometimes we have to spend long boring hours looking for evidence. People behave in ways that constantly surprise us. I respect your judgement, or intuition, whatever you want to call it, but I respectfully suggest you enjoy our triumph, for the time being at least, until some senior officer steals the credit from us.'

They arrived at Delyse's house and Rossi steered the Lancia into her drive and stopped the engine. Delyse did not move. She said, 'The front room light is on.'

'So, perhaps your dad is still up.'

'He never stays up this late.'

'Perhaps he just forgot to switch off the light.'

'He switches everything off before he goes to bed, including the television and kettle. Be safe and save money is his mantra.' They got out and Delyse unlocked the front door. The hallway was dark. 'Dad,' she called. 'Are you still up?'

No reply.

Rossi whispered, 'Let me go in the living room first, just in case.' He pushed open the door to see Eldon Joseph sitting on a dining chair at the table. His mouth was sealed by duct tape and his wrist duct taped together behind his back.

Delyse cried, 'Dad!' and went over to take the tape from his mouth. As she did so Colonel Hugh Latimer stepped in from the kitchen. He was carrying a bottle of whisky in one hand and pointing a revolver with the other. He said, 'I've been waiting for you two interfering fuckers. Where have you been?'

Rossi said, 'We've been destroying your absurd little plot to kill the Prime Minister.'

Latimer laughed. 'That's what you think.'

Eldon said, 'Never mind the Prime Minister. This bastard is drinking my best whisky. Do you know him?'

'Yes, dad. His name is Latimer and he is the Deputy Lord Lieutenant of Bedfordshire.'

'So what is he doing in our house?'

Latimer said, 'I've escaped the clutches of Turnbull and his Special Branch goons. Your daughter and his greasy half Italian friend have fucked up my life and they're going to be my get out of jail free card. You two, sit down at the

148

table and don't move.' He waved the pistol. 'This is my trusty Webley service revolver from my Second World War days. At this range it could blow your head off. I know because I killed many Germans with it when we took Berlin in 1945.'

Rossi said, 'The Red Army took Berlin.'

'I know. That's how I came to admire their courage and tenacity, and why I decided to help them by passing any useful information I could. I was eighteen years old and saw the destruction wreaked by the evil Nazi fascist regime and decided it takes a nation like the Soviet Union to stop such aggression.'

'So you've been a traitor since 1945?' Rossi asked.

'If you like. The zeks plot was to be my greatest service to the Soviet regime, the culmination of my loyalty to the cause.'

Delyse said, 'Killing Mrs Thatcher won't change anything. Some other Conservative will take over and be even more antagonistic against Russia. Besides, Commander Turnbull, his Special Branch team and half the police force of Lancashire are on their way to Blackpool to stop the attack. Put the gun down and we'll put in a good word for you.'

Latimer swayed drunkenly and laughed. 'Turnbull and his team in Blackpool! Wrong end of the country.'

'What do you mean?' Rossi asked.

'You don't think Berisov told you the truth, do you? Turnbull thought he was so clever, capturing Berisov and getting him to betray details of the plot.'

'What about that phone call he made saying the plot had be blown?'

'That was a pre-arranged signal meaning that the British authorities knew about a plot, but the deception had put them on completely the wrong track and it was safe to go ahead with the real plot.'

'What is the real plot?' Delyse asked.

Latimer took a swig of whisky and grinned. 'Wouldn't you like to know? That's why I'm here. Now we're all going to get in that fancy Italian car that Luigi here drives and take me to the nearest ferry port.'

'You're crazy,' Rossi said. 'You're drunk and you'll have to sleep sometime before we even get near a ferry port.'

'I was an army officer for thirty years. I'm used to staying awake, for days if necessary.'

'What a distinguished career you had,' Delyse said. 'Betraying your comrades and marrying for money. You really are a piece of shit.'

Latimer lurched towards Delyse. 'You mind your mouth and your manners you black bitch.'

Latimer's back was momentarily turned to Eldon. With a speed and power belying his years, Eldon brought up his tethered legs and kicked Latimer in the small of the back.

Rossi saw what Eldon was about to do. As Latimer crashed forward he leapt up and grabbed Latimer's gun arm. The pistol fired into the ceiling but Rossi wrenched the pistol away, breaking one of Latimer's fingers. Delyse picked up the whisky bottle and smashed it down on Latimer's head.

As Latimer lay groaning Eldon said, 'You talk to my daughter with respect, you arrogant traitor.'

'Nicely put, father. We had better treat Latimer's head. That's a nasty cut there.'

'And see if you can find the duct tape he used,' Rossi added, as he unwound the tape from Eldon's ankles and arms.

Latimer was weeping. It was obvious he had wet himself.

'He's a broken man,' Eldon said, with a surprising hint of sympathy. 'I've seen it many times in the police force. He'll co-operate now.'

Eldon and Rossi lifted Latimer into an armchair. Rossi tied his legs with duct tape while Delyse treated the bottle wound and Eldon covered Latimer with his own revolver.

Rossi pulled up a chair and sat down in front of Latimer. He said, 'It's over, Colonel. Charlie Falconer isn't coming to your rescue, neither is anyone else. You're only hope for leniency is co-operating with us and Special Branch and tell us, truthfully, everything you know. Tell us now. Do you agree?'

Latimer nodded. He was mumbling incoherently.

Delyse examined Latimer's broken finger and said, 'What did you mean earlier about Berisov's deception and Turnbull and his team being at the wrong end of the country?'

'The Russian bastards deceived me as well,' Latimer slurred drunkenly. 'They used my loathing of Thatcher. She was never their target.'

'Who or what was?' Rossi asked.

'That Labour man, that Neil Kinnock.'

'Neil Kinnock? Leader of the Labour Party? But he's a Socialist. Why would the Soviets want to eliminate a Socialist ally?'

Latimer laughed. 'The Soviet leadership are not Socialists, they are hard line Communists. They want a hard line Communist running Britain. They thought they had a Communist stooge with the former Labour leader, that Michael Foot chap, but he was a political disaster. Kinnock is eminently electable but he is trying to purge his party of the hard line Communists, the so-called Militant Tendency. The Soviets sent the zeks to assassinate Kinnock. It was a no lose situation for the Soviets. If the zeks fail, no harm done to Russia, but if they succeed the British Labour Party might elect a closet Communist fellow traveller, of which there are very many in the Labour Party, as leader.'

Delyse said, 'Give us details of the actual plot. When is it? What's going to happen?'

Latimer mumbled something, his head fell forward and it looked as if he was sleeping. Delyse gently tweaked his broken finger. Latimer came wide awake in pain.

'Sorry to do that,' Delyse said, 'but you must tell us the truth.'

Latimer sighed. 'The plot was brought forward to tomorrow, which actually is today. The Labour Party annual conference begins at noon. Before the main conference opens, Kinnock is making an address in a smaller venue, a meeting room off the main concourse of the centre. The zeks are to infiltrate this meeting, or break in or do whatever they can to kill Kinnock.'

'What time does this address start?'

'Nine.'

Rossi looked at his watch. 'It's three a.m. already.'

'Where is this conference?' Delyse asked.

It was Eldon who answered. 'It's in Bournemouth. On the south coast, I saw it on the news today.'

Latimer nodded. 'Nothing you can do to stop it now. Berisov's deception has worked.'

Rossi stood up. 'I'll ring Turnbull.'

'He's up in Blackpool,' Latimer sniggered.

'I'll get hold of Special Branch, then I'll ring our respective superiors and get their authority to stop the Kinnock meeting.'

'Excellent idea,' Latimer chortled. 'Good luck with that.'

'Eldon, may I use your phone. I might get your telephone bill up a bit higher than normal.'

'Of course,' Eldon said. 'Do whatever you have to do?'

Rossi went out to the hall, where the phone table was placed, and returned seconds later. 'Colonel Latimer here has damaged the plug in jack. No chance of it working. We have to get to a phone. Where is the nearest police station?'

Delyse said, 'That would be headquarters in town where I work. That would mean a lot of questions if I walk in there.'

'I could go in and flash my warrant card.'

Eldon asked, 'How long would it take to persuade the powers-that-be that you are genuine and sincere? From my experience as a senior officer Kinnock will be long dead by the time they accept your story.'

'Dad's right,' Delyse said. 'I've got a better idea. Let's go there and stop it in person. Its five hours before Kinnock speaks. Bournemouth is an easy route, A10, M25, M3. It's a three hour drive at most, especially in the dead of night like as now.'

'I like it,' Rossi said. 'My trusty Lancia will eat up those roads in no time. And, thanks to Latimer, we have a weapon.'

'Wait a minute,' Delyse said, 'we can't leave dad here unarmed with this maniac.'

'Don't you worry about me, girl. I've got the measure of this piece of trash. He caught me by surprise the first time. He won't do it again.'

Delyse said, 'Okay, but as soon as we're clear we'll ring the police and tell them you're holding an intruder. We can sort the inevitable questions about his injuries later.'

Rossi said, 'Delyse, you take the Webley. You are weapons trained. Eldon, watch that nasty bastard like a hawk. I want to talk more cricket with you when we've sorted out this mess.'

153

31

When Delyse woke up the day was dawning. She was surprised to find the car was speeding along a narrow road with woodland all around. She sat up and tried to shake herself awake. 'I'm sorry, Clif, I nodded off.'

'No problem,' Rossi said. 'The nap will do you good. A rest before the upcoming confrontation.'

'Where are we? I thought it was motorway and main road all the way to Bournemouth.'

'We're in the historic New Forest. I've taken to the minor roads. I know them well from when we had family holidays down here. This route will take us straight into Bournemouth without getting caught up in early works traffic.'

'What's the time?'

'Nearly seven o'clock. We'll arrive at the Bournemouth International Conference Centre in about an hour. That will give us another hour to persuade our police colleagues that we are not insane. Hopefully we can get hold of Commander Turnbull to verify our story.'

'And what if they don't believe us?'

Rossi shrugged. 'Then we'll have to arrest the zeks ourselves.'

'You and me and an old World War Two revolver to apprehend four or five zeks?'

'You're up for it, aren't you, sergeant?'

'Guess I'll have to be. What's that funny smell?'

'Steady on, I haven't been able to shower today.'

'Not you, you idiot. And why is there smoke coming from under the dashboard?'

'What?' Rossi cried, but before he could brake there was the hideous noise of crunching metal from under the bonnet.

The bonnet lid flew up and out spouted plumes of smoke from the engine. Rossi managed to steer the stricken car off the road without hitting a tree. 'We better get out,' he said, 'in case it catches fire.'

They climbed out and, after allowing most of the smoke to clear, gingerly peered into the engine compartment. It was obvious the Lancia was going no further without major repairs. Delyse took her shoulder bag out of the car and went to look up and down the narrow country road. 'Nothing and nobody,' she pronounced. 'It was a brilliant idea of yours to get off the main roads.'

'We have to get to a phone or find alternative transport,' Rossi said.

'I'm sorry but I forgot to pack my magic wand.'

'How much change have you got?'

'What for?'

'The phone of course.'

'And where's the call box? No, I haven't got any change. We left in rather a hurry.'

'You must have a phone card?'

'Sorry. Perhaps we can light a fire and use smoke signals.'

'We'll have to hitchhike if we see any traffic.'

'You mean a dishevelled black girl and white man thumbing a lift in the early morning miles from anywhere. Would you stop?'

Rossi sank down to his haunches. 'I've blown it, haven't I. Kinnock begins his speech in less than two hours.'

'Listen, if we can find a phone we can ring Bournemouth constabulary and explain the situation.'

'It's our only chance,' agreed Rossi, 'but you know how these big events, especially political events, attract all sorts of nutters and hoax calls. If I remember rightly there's some sort of camping site down the road. We could perhaps find a phone, or even a lift, there.'

'How far?'

'Two or three miles.'

Four miles and seventy minutes later they arrived at Garton Campsite. It was a wide grassy field enclosed by low hedges and accessed through a farm gate. There were only six tents pitched and no vehicles to be seen. A camper, thankfully wearing a beach towel, came out of the brick-built ablutions block and looked at them curiously.

'Excuse me,' Delyse said. 'Is there a telephone we could use? Our car broke down.'

'I think there's a telephone in the manager's office but I'm not sure.'

'Where's the manager's office?'

The camper pointed to a small wooden hut near the edge of the field.

'What about a car? Could we borrow one?' Rossi asked.

'No cars here. This campsite is for cyclists only. You'll be able to get the bus into Bournemouth later on. It stops outside here at ten o'clock.'

'Brilliant!' Delyse exclaimed. 'Well done, Clifton. We've just walked miles to find a campsite with no cars!'

Rossi, trying to hide his discomfiture, looked at the hut. He asked the camper, 'Is the manager in?'

'No, he doesn't show up until nine, sometimes later.'

'Okay, thank you,' Rossi said. Then to Delyse, 'Our only chance is the manager's hut. There must be a telephone in there.'

They walked over to the hut and tried the door. It was padlocked. Delyse went around to the side and looked through a window. There was a desk and a telephone directly below the window. She looked around for something heavy and selected a fallen tree branch. She smashed the window, put her hand inside and released the window catch. When Rossi arrived to see what all the noise was about, Delyse was already climbing through the window. 'Come on,' she said. 'Here's a phone.'

Rossi climbed in after her, clumsily knocking books and papers off the desk.

'Rotten sneak thief you'd make,' Delyse said.

They found a local telephone directory and looked up the number for the Bournemouth International Conference Centre. Delyse said, 'Let's ring the BICC first, then the police.'

Rossi did not respond.

'Do you want me to do it?' Delyse reached for the phone but Rossi held back her arm. 'I've had an idea,' he said. 'What is the quickest way to get a building evacuated or surrounded by armed response teams?'

'What do I win if I guess right? A cuddly toy?'

'The Irish Republican Army,' Rossi said. 'If the police get a bomb threat from the IRA they have to act.'

'That's true,' Delyse nodded, 'but there is a system of code words issued from time to time by the IRA. If the threat is not reinforced with the right code word, it might not be taken seriously.'

'You're right. The latest code word is given only to senior officers of Chief Superintendent and above. Luckily I know a Chief Superintendent and, thanks to our cricket team, I know his home number. He was bailed and will be taken into custody next week.'

'You mean Pritchard? Why should he co-operate with you after we've virtually brought him down.'

'He brought himself down by going bent.' Rossi picked up the phone and dialled the number. Eventually the phone was answered. Rossi said, 'Hello, Mrs Pritchard. I'm sorry to disturb you so early but it's a matter of the utmost importance that I speak to Chief Superintendent Pritchard immediately. Yes, I know, and I regret what has happened but, believe me, this is a matter of life or death.'

After a few seconds Pritchard came on the line. He said, 'Clifton, why should I help you?'

'Call it expiation, if you like, but the train of events that you set in motion is going to result in the assassination of the Labour Party leader and perhaps the deaths of several bystanders.' Rossi explained the situation.

'So, what can I do about that?'

'You can give me the latest IRA code word so I can get the venue cleared in time.'

'That code word is for senior officers only, *sergeant*.'

'You were a bloody good copper for years. Give me this and I'll do what I can with Special Branch and the Chief Constable to save your career and reputation, and get you a lighter sentence at your trial.'

There was silence.

Rossi thought, 'Come on, come on, for God's sake!'

Eventually Pritchard said, 'The code word is "honeycomb".'

Rossi replaced the handset and said to Delyse, 'Honeycomb is the code word. I'll ring Bournemouth nick first. That will give them an hour to get a SWAT team on site and warn the BICC.' He dialled 999 and, in a cod Irish accent, said, 'This is an official warning from the Irish Provisional Army. A group of armed gunmen intend to assassinate Neil Kinnock at his side meeting in the Marlow Suite at 9 a.m. These men are extremely dangerous. Tell your senior officers that the code word is "honeycomb". Repeat "honeycomb".'

As Rossi put the phone down they heard the rattle of the padlock being unlocked outside. The door opened and a swarthy middle-aged man said, 'What the hell are you doing in my office?'

32

The green and cream coloured single decker bus trundled into the outskirts of Bournemouth. The sun had risen into a cloudless blue sky, a warm Indian summer day. Rossi looked out of the window and, through the trees, caught a glimpse of the sea. It reminded him of the excitement of arriving on holiday when he was a kid. He and his brother could not wait to run on to the sand and splash about in the sea. Despite his poignant memory of his brother and misgivings about whether he had done enough to stop the attempt on Neil Kinnock's life, he felt a serenity and happiness he had not experienced for years. He was cocooned in the warm interior of the bus, the chugging rhythm of the engine, the smells of metal and upholstery, freed from the necessity to do his duty, even if he had so wanted.

Delyse was asleep, her head resting on his shoulder. He looked at her and understood the source of his new-found serenity.

Delyse woke up and realised she was sleeping on Rossi's shoulder. 'Oh, sorry,' she said, sitting up straight. 'I didn't mean to nod off again and use you as a pillow.'

'You're more than welcome,' Rossi said.

'Where are we?'

'Just coming into Bournemouth.'

'It was nice of that camp site manager to lend us the bus fare. Musn't forget to pay him back. What's the time?'

'Half past ten. We should arrive outside the conference centre in about ten minutes.'

'Then we'll know if we've done enough.'

Rossi looked out of the window. 'Everywhere looks calm. No hint of a major incident. No blue lights flashing up and down the promenade.'

'Lovely day,' Delyse said. 'Nice beach. Look at all those normal people being happy and enjoying themselves. Why did we pick this bloody job we do.'

'Because it's us, it's what we are, and we wouldn't be the same without it.'

The bus halted at the stop outside the conference centre. Rossi and Delyse got off and walked towards the massive structure. The entrance was at the top of a long and wide flight of concrete steps. There were many people moving in and out, including several uniformed policemen and women.

'What do you think?' Rossi asked.

'It's busy but no signs of panic or trauma. Let's go inside.'

They climbed the steps and went inside to the spacious foyer. There were people milling around, including several uniformed police, but everything seemed to be under control.

Delyse said, 'There's a Chief Super over there. He seems to be in command. Let's find out what's happened. Get your warrant card out.'

They walked up to the Chief Superintendent. Delyse said, 'Excuse me sir, we are police officers and we wondered if we could assist in anyway.' They showed him their warrant cards.

'Umm, Bedfordshire and Hertfordshire,' the Chief Superintendent mused. 'What makes you think something is wrong?'

Rossi said, 'We are here on holiday, sir, and we couldn't help noticing the flurry of activity. What's happened?'

The Chief Super debated with himself whether to tell them. 'Well, he decided, 'if you must know, there was an IRA plot to assassinate Mr Kinnock at one of his meetings.'

'Really,' Delyse said. 'They planted a bomb?'

'No, they planted a group of five armed men ready to shoot Mr Kinnock. Thanks to a telephone tip-off we were able to deploy an armed response team very quickly. They were on hand because of all the political bigwigs gathered here.'

'So you've detained these armed men?' Rossi asked.

'Yes. Funny thing is, they all seem to be Russian or eastern European rather than Irish. I'm not surprised because the IRA man who phoned in the tip-off had the worst Irish accent I've ever heard. I'd love to know who these gunmen are and what was going on.'

'Perhaps we can help,' Rossi said. 'You see, we. . .'

'I don't see how you can help,' the Chief Super interrupted with a supercilious tone.

'No,' Delyse said, 'what my colleague meant was we can explain. . .'

'Thank you but no, sergeant. Bournemouth and Dorset constabulary have the situation well in hand. We'll soon find out what these men were up to. We don't need help from provincial plod. Go away and enjoy your holiday.' He started to walk away.

'We could save you a lot of time,' Delyse called after him. She made to follow the Chief Super but Rossi held her back. He said, 'Let the arrogant twit waste his time. All that matters is that the zeks have been stopped and arrested. We'll inform Commander Turnbull. He will cut that haughty Chief Super down to size.'

Delyse and Rossi left the conference centre, walked down the steps and stood looking at the wide golden beach and the murmuring sea. 'What do we do now?' Delyse asked. 'I can smell ice cream. Can we get one?'

'No money,' Rossi replied. 'I'll have to arrange to get my car picked up and fixed. That'll take a few days. I might as well stay down here, have a holiday. What are you going to do?'

'I'll ring dad, make sure he's okay. I like your idea of a holiday. I think we've earned it.'

Rossi nodded then realised what Delyse had said. 'Do you mean you'd like to spend the holiday with me?'

Delyse shrugged. 'You can be an irritating and unpredictable sod, obsessed with that bloody car of yours and looking like a dandy in those tailored suits, but you're a good and honest copper and an equally good man. I've sort of gotten used to you. I shouldn't admit it but I missed you like crazy when they split us up.'

'I missed you. You can be a sarcastic, suspicious and domineering sod but I must be a masochist. I enjoy your company. You are also kind, generous, courageous, a great detective and drop dead gorgeous. What's not to like?'

'Holiday it is then,' Delyse smiled. 'One little snag, we haven't brought anything with us, clothes or anything. I'll get dad to send us some money.'

'Good idea. We can buy anything we need. I always take too much on holiday anyway.'

'Are you hungry?'

'Not really,' Rossi said. 'I could do with a good sleep.'

'Shall we find a hotel? I want a room with a sea view.'

'Good luck with that. With all these politicians in town you'll be lucky to get any sort of room. Let's walk towards the outskirts and try a few hotels, see what vacancies they have.' They started walking but Rossi suddenly stopped.

'What's wrong,' Delyse asked.

'I've just remembered that my ex-wife and her new boyfriend came down here to run a hotel. I don't want to stay in theirs.'

Delyse laughed. 'That would be awkward.'

'Especially after what I said to Jane about Bournemouth being a dull geriatric town. On a day like today with the sunlight sparkling off the sea, it's delightful.'

'Perhaps we've turned into dull geriatrics?'

Rossi looked at Delyse smiling at him. He said, 'I've never known anyone less dull or so full of vitality.'

Delyse took his arm as they walked on.

At the fifth time of hotel asking they enquired at the South Cliff Hilton. To their relief the receptionist said, 'Yes, we have rooms with sea views available. Have you any luggage?'

'It's being sent on tomorrow. This is a kind of last minute work thing,' Rossi explained.

'That's fine. Do you want two singles or a double?'

Rossi said, 'Err, two singles, I guess.'

Delyse kissed his cheek and said playfully, 'Oh, stop pretending we are simply colleagues, Clifton. I would be a lot happier with a double, if that's okay with you.'

'Okay?' Rossi smiled. 'That is simply perfect.'

Printed in Great Britain
by Amazon

31451043R00096